"You may, ah, kiss the bride now."

Elisa's bubble burst. Even the Ranger looked startled when he turned to her, his gray eyes roaming desperately from his grandmother to Elisa. She could have sworn his grandmother was holding her breath, love shining in her eyes as she waited for her grandson's big moment.

Elisa might have let the moment pass as Del gave her a perfunctory kiss that served as a reminder that theirs was only a partnership, but she couldn't stand seeing the woman's confusion.

Without daring to contemplate the consequences, she reached up and pulled him down for a real kiss.

It was as if a door unlocked inside Elisa, the entrance to a place she'd closed off long ago. The place that was feminine and sensual.

Suddenly she wasn't kissing the Ranger to please his grandmother. This was all for herself. And the sense that finally, *finally*, she didn't have to be the strong one any longer.

Dear Reader,

Our exciting month of May begins with another of bestselling author and reader favorite Fiona Brand's Australian Alpha heroes. In *Gabriel West: Still the One*, we learn that former agent Gabriel West and his ex-wife have spent their years apart wishing they were back together again. And their wish is about to come true, but only because Tyler needs protection from whoever is trying to kill her—and Gabriel is just the man for the job.

Marie Ferrarella's crossline continuity, THE MOM SQUAD, continues, and this month it's Intimate Moments' turn. In *The Baby Mission*, a pregnant special agent and her partner develop an interest in each other that extends beyond police matters. Kylie Brant goes on with THE TREMAINE TRADITION with *Entrapment*, in which wickedly handsome Sam Tremaine needs the heroine to use the less-than-savory parts of her past to help him capture an international criminal. Marilyn Tracy offers another story set on her Rancho Milagro, or Ranch of Miracles, with *At Close Range*, featuring a man scarred—inside and out—and the lovely rancher who can help heal him. And in Vickie Taylor's *The Last Honorable Man*, a mother-to-be seeks protection from the man she'd been taught to view as the enemy—and finds a brand-new life for herself and her child in the process. In addition, Brenda Harlan makes her debut with *McIver's Mission*, in which a beautiful attorney who's spent her life protecting families now finds that *she* is in danger—and the handsome man who's designated himself as her guardian poses the greatest threat of all.

Enjoy! And be sure to come back next month for more of the best romantic reading around, right here in Intimate Moments.

Leslie J. Wainger
Executive Senior Editor

Please address questions and book requests to:
Silhouette Reader Service
U.S.: 3010 Walden Ave., P.O. Box 1325, Buffalo, NY 14269
Canadian: P.O. Box 609, Fort Erie, Ont. L2A 5X3

The Last Honorable Man

VICKIE TAYLOR

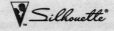

INTIMATE MOMENTS™

Published by Silhouette Books

America's Publisher of Contemporary Romance

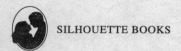 **SILHOUETTE BOOKS**

ISBN 0-373-27293-6

THE LAST HONORABLE MAN

Visit Silhouette at www.eHarlequin.com

Printed in U.S.A.

Books by Vickie Taylor

VICKIE TAYLOR

has always loved books—the way they look, the way they feel and most especially the way the stories inside them bring whole new worlds to life. She views her recent transition from reading to writing books as a natural extension of this longtime love. Vickie lives in Aubrey, Texas, a small town dubbed "The Heart of Horse Country," where, in addition to writing romance novels, she raises American quarter horses and volunteers her time to help homeless and abandoned animals. Vickie loves to hear from readers. Write to her at: P.O. Box 633, Aubrey, TX 76227.

To Ann Leslie Tuttle, editor extraordinaire, for her unswerving faith and consummate professionalism. Thanks for everything!

Chapter 1

Mine honour is my life; both grow in one;
Take honour from me, and my life is done.
—Shakespeare, King Richard II Act 1, sc. 1

Silence gathered in the wake of gunfire.

Sergeant Del Cooper straightened from his shooting crouch, tugged his Stetson low on his forehead to block the glare of the August sun and hitched the stock of his shotgun up tight under his damp armpit.

So much for Sunday being the day of peace.

Squaring his shoulders, he rose from behind the old Buick he'd used as cover. One by one the others appeared from the shadows of shallow doorways and behind the stoops of dull gray industrial buildings, stepping into sunlight so bright their silhouettes blurred in a hazy glow. The four of them met in the middle of the road and strode forward together, their booted heels scuffing the long shadows cast on the blacktop in front of them. A crimson stain slashed across Hayes's sleeve, but at least they were all on their feet. Del doubted the men in the warehouse at the other end of the road could say the same.

Overhead, an outraged shriek broke the quiet. Del tipped his head back. Squinting against the sun's brilliance, he watched a blackbird circle between the crisp, blue sky and the pewter clouds of gun smoke hanging low over the street, their sulfurous fumes burning his nose and throat. The bird offered another raucous challenge, swooping to defend his territory.

"Sorry, fella," Del said. "The fightin's all over."

A bead of sweat squeezed past his hatband and rolled toward the corner of his eye. He wiped it away with the sleeve of his duster. The cowboy coat's long hem swished and swirled around his calves. It was too hot for any kind of jacket this time of year in Dallas, but the long coat covered the shotgun when Del snugged the barrel up against his thigh, and Del hadn't wanted the weapon to draw attention to himself or his teammates.

Huh. As if anyone with half a mind wouldn't take one look at them and see trouble coming.

From his position on the end, he glanced down the line at the others. At an imposing six foot four and nearly two hundred lean pounds, Captain "Bull" Matheson set the pace from the right-center spot in the row, his left hand resting on the butt of the Colt holstered at his hip. To the captain's right, with handgun still drawn, dangling loose but ready at his side, wiry-bodied Clint Hayes kept pace, somber faced and silent. Only Solomon, the diminutive new kid next to Del, with her six-shooter stretched in front of her in a white-knuckled grip, had the wild-eyed look of the untried.

"Some of 'em got away," she said, breathless.

He spared her a glance. Katherine "Kat" Solomon's eyes were bright, jumpy. "Some of 'em didn't."

"You got one."

"Yeah." He shifted the Remington twelve-gauge so that the barrel rested in the crook of his arm and concentrated on keeping his legs steady beneath him. All of a sudden his knees felt as if they had more joints than they ought. "I got one."

It was days like this—days when the adrenaline rushed through his veins like a swollen river one moment, then dried up like bones in a desert the next, leaving him shaky and perspiring—that he felt the full weight of the badge on his chest. The silver circle and star carried a responsibility. A tradition. A code of honor that demanded he right wrongs, defend the defenseless. And sometimes that he take a life.

But never that he take satisfaction in it.

He knew the kid hadn't meant anything. She just hadn't learned yet that they didn't talk about it afterward. Those demons were to be faced later, in private. It was part of the code. Besides, this wasn't over yet; they still had to clear that warehouse.

They'd nearly reached the front of the building, and still no sign of life. Del doubted there would be. A loose piece of tin on the roof creaked in the hot breeze. A scrap of litter kicked up from the street, swirled and danced in front of them, then skittered out of their path.

Captain Matheson motioned to Hayes. "Side entrance." Then he looked at Del. "Back door."

"I'll take the back door," Solomon chirped, her voice tight as a high wire.

She was already moving when Matheson scowled and

called her back. "Hold on there, Johnette Wayne. You're on the front, with me."

Solomon's expression soured to downright mutinous, but she didn't argue. At least not out loud.

Del watched curiously as the two of them measured each other. "Bull" Matheson was always hard on the new kids at first, but Solomon had been with them nearly a month now, and the sparks between her and the Bull showed no signs of letting up. If Del didn't know better, he'd think it was something personal between them.

Matheson turned to Del. "Take the big gun to the back door," he said. "We'll flush, you catch."

Unlike Solomon, Del didn't even think about arguing. Hefting the shotgun to his shoulder, he trotted around the building, careful to stay low and out of the line of fire from the windows. He didn't think anything—anyone—was still alive in there, but it never hurt to be cautious, especially since the angle of the sun on this side of the building cast a glare on the grimy glass, making it more difficult to spot movement inside.

He'd taken position behind a stack of wooden pallets at the rear of the warehouse when he caught a flash of color behind him and to his right. He wasn't sure what it was, but it shouldn't be there.

His throat dried up as another shot of adrenaline hit his system. He needed to focus on what might be coming out that back door, but he didn't like the thought of one of them behind him. He caught another flash of movement among the stacks of pallets. Just a shadow this time, but something nonetheless—and coming his way.

With a glance at the warehouse, seeing nothing moving inside, he made his decision. Matheson might have his hide for leaving his position, but if one of the shooters was out here, Del couldn't let him get away.

He crept along the concrete walls of the docks, searching. Listening. He was crouching beneath a rusted iron staircase, about to poke his head up and look around when a whirlwind descended on him from above. Caught in a vortex of colors—vibrant red and orange, warm brown and stormy blue—he thrashed. Gauzy fabric snarled around him, hemmed him in, and he rolled, trying to get free and hold onto the shotgun at the same time.

He twisted for better leverage, his body molded around a warm and solid human form, struggling mightily. He turned again until he was on top of the bucking body, and his hands let go of the gauze and twisted in something long and soft before he opened his eyes—

—and found himself staring down at one of the most naturally beautiful women he'd ever seen. Earthy, yet exotic, her complexion was the color of toasted almond, smooth and perfect, except for charcoal smudges under her lashes that said it had been too long since she'd slept. Perfectly pitched eyebrows arched over eyes the color of sweet, dark chocolate and her hair… It was long and smooth and black as coffee—a rich, Colombian roast—and felt like pure silk wrapped in his fists.

He jerked his hands away.

For a moment she lay there, wide-eyed and frozen. The V-neck blouse she wore had come untied at the throat. With each heaving breath she drew, the thrust of her chest pried the slit farther apart and exposed another centimeter of lustrous flesh.

Reining in his galloping pulse—and his imagination—Del reassured her. "It's all right, ma'am. I'm a—"

She moved fast. Hard. She fought like a hellcat, flailing her fists and kicking. Del had to roll to the side to protect the parts of him that Kevlar couldn't cover. They both lunged to their feet and she nearly got away, but her full skirt tangled around her legs, slowing her. She dropped a military-style olive green backpack, the drawstring kind women used as a purse sometimes, and Del kicked it away in case there was a weapon inside, then managed to snag her with an arm around her waist.

She squirmed in his grasp and tried to stomp his instep with her heel. Amazon woman just didn't know when to give up. He dodged blows and held on for all he was worth. Her arms and legs were long and lean—she was fit, no doubt about that. But her middle was solid. Thick, almost bulging in a way it shouldn't be unless—

Holy Mother.

He let go of her as if he'd reached into a pile of wood for a walking stick and pulled back a rattlesnake instead.

Big mistake.

He knew what was coming when she wrapped the palm of one hand around the fist of the other and raised her elbows, but it happened so fast there was nothing he could do to prevent it.

He had to admire her spirit. The fact that he stood a half foot taller, weighed a good fifty pounds more and was armed—with a shotgun, no less—didn't seem to faze her. The elbow she buried in his gut doubled him over like a Gumby doll. The heel she stomped on the arch of his foot nearly buckled his knees. If she'd weighed more, she'd have done him some serious damage with the combat boots she wore under her skirt. He supposed he was lucky on that account, at least.

While he stood there gagging and hopping, she took off.

Toward the warehouse.

That was all he needed, Amazon woman running around in there. Even if the shooters who'd survived had cleared out—which wasn't a certainty—she could run into Solomon. The hair-triggered new kid was wound tight enough to pop anything that moved. And Amazon woman was definitely moving. She'd already cleared half the distance to the warehouse, the leather soles of her boots slapping the ground as she ran.

"Wait," he called, still gasping for air. "You can't go in there. It's danger—" Ah, great. She wasn't listening. Ignoring the pain in his ribs and his foot, he took off after her.

Del cursed when she disappeared into the back door of the building. This was a disaster in the making. If she jumped one of his teammates the way she'd jumped him, she just might find herself closely acquainted with a few .38 caliber slugs.

He reached the door and pried it open. Going inside would be just about as dangerous for him. The others wouldn't be expecting him in there. If they mistook him for one of the black-clad bad guys...

Pushing that thought out of his mind, he slipped through the door. The cool interior made his skin, flushed with sweat from the hand-to-hand skirmish, turn clammy. His heart tattooed a rapid pace. He couldn't see the woman, but he picked up the faint pad of her steps on the floor behind a row of crates ahead.

He crept toward the sound, his gaze flicking side to side, watching for his teammates, and for the shooters. He didn't dare call out, in case any of them were still around.

The woman's light footsteps halted, somewhere around the end of the row of crates, Del guessed. Holding his breath, he moved toward her. He'd almost caught up to her when a shadow crawled along the floor to his left—a pair of outstretched arms and a gun. Solomon's body followed the shadow, swinging around to where the woman stood.

Swallowing his curse, Del stepped between the two women. His forearm shot up, knocking Solomon's aim toward the ceiling. An explosion roared from the muzzle of the gun. He felt the blast of heat on his cheek, saw the flash of light. The pistol's report deafened him for a second, then set bells ringing in his head. That had been too close.

Amazon woman recovered before he did, but then, she hadn't just nearly had her head blown off. She whirled, her eyes huge, then ran.

Del chased her again, this time with Solomon two steps behind. To hell with giving away their position. He shouted, "Hold your fire, we have a civilian in the building!"

As he neared the end of a row of crates and pulled up to round the corner, an anguished wail stopped him in his tracks. Solomon, who'd been running on his heels, crashed into his back, then they both started to run again, pulled forward by the keening.

Del and his teammates converged on the scene at once, weapons ready. Hayes, his revolver trained on the downed form of one of the gunmen in black, yelled, "Clear."

But Del wasn't looking at the dead gunman. Or at the open boxes of weapons—a cache like he'd never seen before: automatic rifles, handguns, shotguns, even hand-held air-to-ground missile launchers that could bring down a small plane—surrounding them. He couldn't take his eyes off the sight a few feet beyond, in the center of a cleared section of the warehouse floor. The mystery woman sat on the cement, her long legs curled beneath her skirt, holding a second lifeless body in her arms, moaning softly and rocking the dead man as if he were a child just nodding off to sleep.

Pressure built in Del's chest like water behind a dam as he took in the details. This second man wasn't dressed in dark coveralls like the other gunmen who'd escaped. He wore pressed navy-blue slacks and a white dress shirt, now stained red with blood from a wide wound—the kind of wound only a shotgun blast could cause. A patch on his sleeve identified him as a security guard, working for one of the agencies that protected the warehouse district. This wouldn't be the first time one of the minimum-wage guards had been dealing dirty from his place of employment.

But Del didn't see a gun. Where was the man's gun? There had to be a gun. God, there'd better be one. Had the woman picked it up?

She shifted, rocking herself and the dead man forward again, and the dam in Del's chest burst, sweeping away everything he believed about who he was, what he was. He was nothing. Nobody. Because the man on the floor couldn't have had a gun.

His hands were tied behind his back.

My God, he hadn't been part of the deal going down, but simply a security guard doing his job, taken hostage, maybe, when he walked in on the transaction.

Blood roared in Del's ears, drowning out everything but the woman's cries and his pounding heart. He fell to his knees, his legs no longer capable of supporting him. Pure instinct forced him to press two fingers alongside the column of the man's throat. He tried to recall the prayers he'd learned in childhood, but his brain would only form one word, over and over.

Please, please, please...

He held his fingers over the man's carotid a moment,

with the others looking down on him in silence, then shook his head.

The woman raised her dark chocolate eyes, now glistening, to his, then to each of his companions in turn. To Del's surprise, they showed no trace of the shock that usually accompanied a person's first up close exposure to the vulgar reality of violence, but held instead the knowledge of one all too familiar with death. With loss.

"Federales?" she whispered, her voice thick with tears close to the surface, but not shed.

"No, ma'am." Del let his hand fall away from the body she held. He met the woman's gaze squarely, somehow holding his head high when everything inside him wanted to collapse. "Texas Rangers."

They buried Eduardo Garcia in a pleasant enough spot. There weren't any trees close enough to shade him from the sun in summer, but a flagstone wall screened him from the strip mall next to the cemetery, and it was quiet. At least it was today, with the jets taking off to the south, the opposite direction from the graveyard, out of nearby Dallas/Fort Worth airport. Still, Del couldn't help but wonder if the man didn't deserve better.

The answer came to him harshly. Of course he did; he deserved to still be alive.

Del dug his fists into eyes gritty from lack of sleep and the dust blowing in from West Texas on an arid wind. His chest ached as if something was missing inside him.

As if his soul was gone.

Waiting in the negligible shade of a scrub mesquite on a knoll some hundred yards from the gravesite, he scanned the assemblage of mourners again, still not finding what—who—he was looking for.

Vultures, mostly, had turned out for the service. Reporters. The investigation into exactly what happened at the warehouse was still ongoing. But no connection between Garcia and the gunmen or the confiscated weapons had been found. Word that an innocent man had been shot by one of the legendary Texas Rangers—especially word that an innocent *Hispanic* man had been shot by a Caucasian Texas Ranger—had the press on a witch-hunt.

Unfortunately, Del was the witch.

They were the reason he watched from up here, instead of bowing his head before the preacher. Lay low, Bull had told him. Let this blow over.

At the time he'd thought Captain Matheson meant a day or two, until the inspectors from the Department of Public Safety—the state agency that oversaw the Rangers—finished grilling him about the incident and declared Garcia's death a tragic but unavoidable accident. But five days had passed since the shooting. The medical examiner had released the body after performing a full autopsy, and still the DPS inspectors hadn't made any ruling. The furor showed no signs of dying down any time soon.

It didn't matter. Let the system work its course, he told himself. He could pay his respects to Garcia later, after the press left. It wasn't as if the man was going anywhere.

What mattered today was that *she* wasn't down there, either. Amazon woman. The lady whose cries echoed in his mind a thousand times a night, robbed him of his sleep. The one he'd come to see.

There had been no question who had fired the shot that killed Garcia. Del was the only one carrying a shotgun. Within minutes of finding Garcia, Bull had ordered Del away from the crime scene, and rightly so. The death of a civilian—an innocent man—demanded an unbiased investigation. Del hadn't had the chance to talk to the mystery woman with the dark chocolate eyes. He needed to know more about her. What Garcia had been to her. What Del had taken from her. He needed to know.

He scanned the crowd huddled around the grave once again, skipping over the media with their tripods and film-at-ten television cameras, looking for her.

Why hadn't she come?

Disappointed, he supposed the reporters had kept her away, too. So far, the press hadn't caught on to the fact that Garcia had been involved with a woman. Del hoped it stayed that way. She would be going through enough right now without the press hounding her.

On the plain below, those surrounding the grave, even most of the reporters, lowered their heads in prayer. This far away, Del couldn't hear the words. He didn't need to; he knew them all to well.

Yea, tho I walk through the valley of the shadow of death…

He'd been walking through a valley of his own since the shooting. Five days of reliving the same two-second slice of life over and over.

He crouches behind the car. Windows break in the warehouse across from him. Hayes is on the move, sprinting across the road. Inside the warehouse he sees the figure of a man through a window. The man raises a rifle, tracking Hayes.

Del stands. Fires two rounds from the shotgun.

And then hears the woman's anguished cry, again and again.

Del can't remember ever seeing the hostage. But the windows were dirty. The sun glared off streaked panes then disappeared into the darkness beyond the jagged edges of glass.

He'd had to fire. Done the only thing he could. If he hadn't, Hayes would have been killed.

That didn't make being responsible for an innocent man's death any easier to bear.

Damn it, why hadn't he seen Garcia?

That wasn't the only question that plagued Del. He had others. Like what was Garcia doing there in the first place? Had he been on duty? Who had called in the anonymous tip that had led the rangers to be there at the same time. And who was the woman? Why was she there?

Del had been kept out of the loop in the investigation. The investigators wouldn't tell him anything, except that the woman's story seemed to check out. Elisa Reyes was from a small South American nation called San Ynez. She had only arrived in the U.S. a few hours before the shooting, had gone to Garcia's apartment and then to his work address when she found he wasn't home. She'd gotten to the warehouse just in time to see the gun battle. She didn't seem to know anything about the deal that was supposed to have gone down there.

Del had tried to get more out of the DPS inspectors, but they'd stonewalled him. Matheson hadn't been much more forthcoming. Damn it, it had been nearly a week, and they hadn't cleared him in the shooting yet. The press had declared him a vigilante racist, and no one official was saying anything different.

He'd like to take those reporters to his farm up near Sherman and introduce them to his *abuela,* the grandmother who had raised him. She'd have a thing or two to say about Del's supposed prejudice against Hispanics.

Then again, what she would say about it wouldn't likely be printable.

He almost smiled, picturing her face in mother-hen mode, protecting her chick. Almost. Because as soon as she chased the reporters away, she'd have a thing or two to say to him.

"You're a good boy, Del Cooper, with a good name, an honorable name," she'd always told him. "You do what's right, pay your debts and you'll keep it that way."

He'd tried. For the most part he thought he'd succeeded, until five days ago. He'd done the right thing by shooting. He was sure of it. But now he had a responsibility to the woman at the warehouse. A debt he wasn't sure he could ever pay. He only knew he had to try. He had to pass on his respects for her loss, if nothing else. But first he had to find her.

Down below, the crowd around the gravesite began to break up. Muttering to himself, Del walked back to his Land Rover. Inside, he shoved the car into gear and drove, his mind still on the woman.

What would he have said to her if he had found her? I'm sorry I killed…who? An innocent man? Someone you cared about? But I had no choice. It was a righteous shoot. Righteous…

His throat closing around that final word, Del headed to the back road through the cemetery, winding down a gravel drive to avoid passing the media vultures. This part of the cemetery was older. Century oaks towered over moss-covered headstones and larger monuments. Gnarled branches seemed to shake their fingers at him. The rustle of leaves in the breeze accused him.

Geez, he was really losing it.

He pressed down on the accelerator, spotting a rear

exit to the cemetery, then stomped even harder on the brake. Beneath an aperture in the canopy of boughs sat a weathered chapel, a flagstone path leading from the road to its entrance, where the half-open door had caught his attention. Shutting off the car's engine, he craned his head for a closer look.

Mortar crumbled between the rough-cut stones of the building's facade. A peeling white steeple scraped against the lower branches of the trees, which shifted in the breeze, their rattle sounding less threatening and more inviting here, mixed with chipper birdsong and the scuttle of a lone squirrel pawing through old pine needles.

The place reminded him of the little church near his *abuela's* farm, only smaller yet. He'd spent many hours there as a child, on his knees at her side, and the sudden longing for that simpler time drew him closer. It wasn't until he got to the door that he saw the drawstring backpack on the floor—the same olive green backpack the woman had been carrying at the warehouse.

It appeared he wasn't the only one drawn by the peacefulness of the place.

Elisa Reyes fingered her rosary beads, her lips moving in silent prayer, and inhaled the scent of old, polished wood, wet stone and candle wax. A single flame flickered from a votive on the stone wall beside her. The muted light set the stained-glass image of Christ on a the cross above the altar aglow.

Elisa had come into the chapel seeking a much-needed respite from the heat. Since she had arrived in Texas five days ago, Elisa felt as if she had been consigned to hell. The sun seemed to burn right through her. She was hot. So hot...and dry.

She paused in her prayers a moment to lick her parched lips. A wave of dizziness shook her, and she had to steady herself with a hand on the back of the pew in front of her until the lightheadedness passed. Grateful for the return of her strength, she took comfort in the silence and reverence of the tiny chapel for another second, then bowed her head again to finish her rosary. This place was the first she had found in this country that reminded her of home.

The first place she had found peace.

Until the squeak of hinges announced that she wasn't alone.

Ever so slightly she cocked her head and looked over her shoulder. Through the black lace veil that covered her eyes, she saw the silhouette of a man in the doorway. He was large and dark, seemingly made more of shadow than flesh and bone. If it were not for the bright halo of daylight behind him giving shape to his form, she might not have believed there was a man there at all, no substance. Just a trick of the light. Dark energy.

Then he stepped down the aisle. His boot heels scuffed the worn wood floor. "Ma'am, I'm Del Coo—"

Elisa's back stiffened. Suddenly she was not hot, but cold to the marrow. "I know who you are. Have you come here seeking absolution, Ranger Cooper?"

His throat convulsed. His hands crushed the brim of the Western hat he carried in front of him like a shield. "No, ma'am. I came here seeking you."

Quickly she crossed herself and rose without meeting his eyes. Icy rage lent strength to her weakened body. "Then you have wasted your time. I am not your confessor."

"I have no intention of burdening you with my sins."

She tried to pass him in the aisle, but his muscular mass blocked the narrow passage.

"You weren't at the service," he said. She did not mean to look at him. Had not intended to acknowledge his presence any further. But something in what he said, some pain beneath the words, beneath the throaty baritone voice, called to her, and she looked at him.

His hair was cropped military short. So short that she could not call it brown or black—just dark. He had a broad forehead, but his brows were not overly heavy, and his strong, square jaw compensated. His nose looked as though it had been broken a time or two, and his gaze was not as cold as one might expect from gray eyes, but instead threw her pale reflection back at her like warm, polished pewter.

He had a dependable face, she decided. Sturdy. The kind of face people would trust.

It was too bad she knew it to be a mask. He was no stalwart defender of humanity. He was a cold-blooded killer.

And yet he had been at Eduardo's funeral when she had not. She had lacked the courage to face the newsmen, as well as the strength to walk the last half mile.

The injustice of it enraged her. She raised her chin, digging her nails into her palms to keep her hands from shaking. "I do not have to be at God's side for Him to hear my words. Nor, thanks to you, do I have to be so near to Eduardo now."

The ranger jerked as if he had been slapped. She tried to shoulder past, but he let go of his hat with one hand and captured her arm. "You're pregnant, aren't you?"

The breath whooshed out of her. Up this close, she could see the deep lines of strain that channeled out from the corners of his eyes and mouth. What worries weighed on him? The death of an innocent man? Surely not. He was *policía*. Heartless.

So what did he want with her?

"How do you know about my baby?" she asked.

"I felt it," he ground out as if his jaw were frozen. "When we were wrestling at the warehouse."

She yanked her arm free of his grip and smoothed her hand over her swelling abdomen. "Yes. I carry Eduardo's child. So you see with your carelessness you took not one life, but three—the man, the husband and the father."

This time the ranger didn't flinch. He frowned. "Husband? You were married?"

"We were to be."

His shoulders sagged. He blinked slowly. "I'm sorry. If there was anything I could do…"

She passed by him. This time she would not be stopped. Behind her, he cleared his throat. "I just want you to know you have my sympathy."

She turned in the chapel doorway. "Sympathy from the devil is little comfort, Ranger." Then she stepped over the threshold, into a Texas heat surely hotter than hell.

Del stood still as marble, a testament to the discipline ingrained in him by four years in the Army Special Forces and fourteen as a cop of one sort or another. It took every bit of will he had, and then some, not to place his fist through the pretty little stained-glass panel beside the door.

This was why he'd wanted to see her, he realized. So she could lay him open. Maybe in that way he could honor his debt in one bloody stream instead of paying slowly, drop by drop.

Only, it hadn't worked. Instead of the anger he'd expected from her, he'd gotten only cold contempt, and instead of making payment, he'd found his debt tripled. She'd said he killed three men, and she'd been right. The sheer magnitude of what one pull of the trigger—*his* pull of the trigger—had cost her was incomprehensible.

One thing he did comprehend, though. A debt like that could never be repaid. Never. He closed his eyes. God help him. Maybe he should find a confessional after all.

He stood there for what seemed like a long time, fighting the invisible steel bands squeezing his chest with each breath he drew. He'd done what he had to do, he told himself. Saved Hayes's life.

So why did he feel like he'd committed a mortal sin?

Feeling much older than his thirty-eight years, he finally sighed and managed to uncrimp his fingers from the ruined brim of his hat. He moved toward the door, but before he'd finished a step, a missile of a sharp-tongued woman crashed into his chest, her chocolate eyes wide with alarm.

"What?" he asked, setting her back on her feet. Her shoulders jutted through the thin blouse beneath his hands. She felt frail. Broken inside. But her disdain was intact.

She brushed off his touch as if he was an insect and pushed them both deeper into the stone chapel. "Reporters," she said, checking over her shoulder.

Del leaned around her, looked out the door and cursed. A van with a KDAL logo cruised down the gravel lane. "Where's your car?"

She clutched her pack to her chest. "I don't have one."

Without looking down, he saw in his mind the dust rimming the hem of her black skirt. How far was it from wherever she was staying to the cemetery? The nearest hotel had to be four or five miles. ''You walked?''

She answered by narrowing her eyes, as if pregnant women always walked miles on the highway in 103-degree heat. Saving his disbelief for later, he pulled her back toward the door. ''Come on.''

Her hand was in his just long enough for him to register the clammy feel of her palm. Then she recoiled. He gritted his teeth, motioning for her to go first. ''After you.''

She didn't budge.

''That's my Land Rover out front. We can get away before they make us.''

''I will go nowhere with you.''

The rebuke blew away another chunk of what was left of his self-respect. She needed his help, whether she realized it or not. So far, Garcia's involvement with a woman had been held to speculation. He could only guess she wasn't interested in publicity, otherwise all four local channels would have plastered the face of the grieving fiancée on the TV news every night this week.

''Look,'' he urged. ''The press is still in a feeding frenzy over the shooting. Finding either one of us in here alone would provide a passable story for the bloodsuckers, but finding us here together will make for a regular tabloid extravaganza. Our pictures will be on sale at every grocery store checkout from here to Minnesota. They will hound us—*you*—night and day. Is that what you want?''

Her face paled to the same light ivory as her blouse. ''No.''

He resisted the urge to steady her on her feet, doubting

she'd appreciate the sentiment. Instead he pulled his own shoulders back, hardened his gaze to match hers. "Then what's it going to be, lady? Ready to make a deal with the devil?"

Chapter 2

"Where do you want me to take you?" the ranger asked.

"Just stop the car."

Elisa pressed her forehead against the cool window. Across the six lanes of cement on the other side of the glass, a pasture dotted by mesquite trees and cows with extraordinarily long horns bordered the parking lot of a modern sports stadium with a gigantic hole in the roof. Rural Texas gave way to urban in a dizzying blur.

A big truck sped past, rocking the vehicle. Elisa rested her palm on her churning stomach and looked away. Everything was so different here than in her country. So big. So fast. In her village, two cars couldn't have passed on the main road without scraping door handles, and the normal flow of traffic was foot speed.

Except when the soldiers came.

The hand on her stomach fisted. "Please stop the car."

The ranger's jaw ticked, but his eyes stayed on the

road. The ruddy spots on his cheeks darkened. "I told you, I am not dumping a pregnant woman on the side of the highway in this heat. In any weather, damn it."

"There is no need to curse."

"Curse? What...? 'Damn it'?"

She frowned at him.

"Aw, hell," he muttered, then shot her a look. "I mean heck. Look, just tell me where you want to go and I'll drop you off."

"You don't understand." She clutched her pack to her side. It was all she'd brought to America. All she'd had. "I—"

Too late.

Elisa's eyes went wide as the wave began low in her body and rolled upward. One hand flying to cover her mouth, she fumbled at the window control with the other.

"What the—" The ranger stepped on the brakes and swerved to the shoulder.

Elisa was out before the car came to full stop. At the guardrail, she fell to her knees and lost what little she'd eaten that day. When it was over, she hung across the steel barrier, limp as yesterday's laundry, clammy and shaking. She dragged in a breath of air, tasted exhaust and nearly choked again. Thankfully, the ranger had left her to her peace. The only thing more humiliating than being sick would have been to have him standing over her, watching.

A moment later she realized she'd offered her thanks too soon. Her stomach turned once more at the sound of his boots crunching across gravel. He stopped beside her and a column of shade fell over her where he blocked the sun. Grudgingly she huddled in the cool swath. She should get up, walk away. But she was so hot... "Leave me alone." Her voice sounded miserable. Pitiful.

"I'm afraid I can't do that, ma'am." Refusing to look into the eyes again of the man who had killed Eduardo, she focused on the ground until blunt fingers appeared in front of her face, waving a rumpled napkin sporting a fast-food chain logo.

Loath as she was to accept his help, even in the form of a napkin, her suffering would prove nothing. He was the one who should be shamed by what he had done, not her.

She snatched the thin paper and wiped her face. A plastic bottle of spring water appeared next and she took it, too.

What was the difference? Her pride was already in tatters. Had been since she left her own people to come to America.

The water was warm, but blessedly wet. She swished it around in her mouth and spit over the guardrail.

The ranger cleared his throat. "I guess I should consider myself lucky."

Without meaning to, she raised her head. He had a way of making her forget her intentions, like her vow not to let him see her pain—or her temper—in the chapel.

"Lucky?" she said.

"You have good reason to hate me." He raised one solemn eyebrows. "And I *am* within spitting distance."

The weakness in her body must have weakened her mind, too, because it took her seconds to put together his meaning. By the time she had, her stomach had rolled from her throat to the floor of her abdomen. "Perhaps you will not feel so lucky when you look more closely at your car."

"Good thing I paid the extra hundred bucks for Scotchgard, then."

Thanks to more than eight years of foreign language classes, Elisa's English was good—better than most native speakers, since she'd learned classroom grammar, not street slang. She prided herself on her extensive vocabulary—but she did not know this thing, Scotchgard. An inborn sense of curiosity almost made her ask, but the question was lost in a gasp. She pressed the heel of her hand against her navel, hoping to stem the rising tide of nausea.

This time, she was almost grateful for the distraction the sickness provided. She knew better than to ask questions of him. He was a Texas Ranger.

"Are you all right?" Squatting beside her, the ranger steadied her with a hand under her elbow.

She nodded toward the ground at his feet. "Do you also pay extra to Scotchgard those?"

He followed her gaze down. "My boots? No."

Ostrich, she guessed. Expensive. "Then perhaps you should get them out of 'spitting distance.'"

He quickly shuffled behind her—without letting go of her arm. Within seconds another swell of sickness rolled through her. Her back bowed, crested and then went limp. Her head hung over the gritty metal rail. She tried focusing on the ditch below for stability, but the very earth pitched like the sea. A cry escaped her, and a surge of shame followed as the ranger watched the final purging of her stomach.

A moment later the ground went still again. She opened her eyes as the ranger dug a pack of gum from his shirt pocket, pulled a piece from its paper wrapper, folded the silver foil halfway back and extended it out to her, holding it by the still-wrapped end.

How was he continually able to offer her the one thing she couldn't refuse at the time? Practically snarling, she snapped the gum from his hand. A moment later, with sugar and spearmint sweetening her tongue, she propped her back against the guardrail and drew her knees to her chest. The roiling cauldron in her stomach settled to a slow simmer, but her strength had yet to reappear.

The ranger watched her, muscled thighs straining the seams of his dress slacks as he squatted. "Have you been sick like this much?"

She tipped her head back and squeezed her eyes shut. "Every day. They call it morning sickness, no? But for me it comes in the afternoon."

"How far along are you?"

"Over four months. It should have passed by now." Her voice wobbled. This weakness left her defenseless against the worry she'd been pushing back since she'd learned of her pregnancy. Worry that she didn't know *how* to have a baby.

"You're not showing much for almost five months. But it's different for everyone," he told her, his words gentle, reassuring.

"You have children?" she couldn't resist asking.

"No. But I lived out in the country as a kid. My grandmother was a midwife for half the babies born in Van Zandt county. I grew up listening to her stories."

Memories of Oleda, the eccentric old midwife from Elisa's village, flashed through her mind like a favorite movie. She had not asked Oleda about the sickness before leaving San Ynez; she had not been able to risk it.

She would not risk it when she returned, either. She would bear this baby alone, if she lived to bear it at all. Despite his gentle voice, this ranger was responsible for that.

She looked up at him. His wide shoulders bunched and released under his sports jacket. The light scent of soap and sandalwood wafted to her on a puff of a breeze. The corners of his mouth angled up hopefully, as if he wanted to smile at the newfound peace between them. She had never seen his smile, but could imagine it— warm and beguiling, pulling a matching grin from whomever it fell on. His would be the kind of smile women trusted. The kind they depended on. Wanted to wake up next to.

Suddenly he was too close, too male, too alive. All the things Eduardo had been and was no more.

Once again the ranger had made her forget her intentions. Made her forget who she was, and who he was— *policía.* Untouchable.

Dredging up the energy from deep inside, she rose on rubbery legs. He rose with her, still steadying her. She held the half-full water bottle out to him. He shook his head. "Keep it. You're probably dehydrated."

She dropped the bottle next to his expensive boots, and the smile that had been so close to breaking, died, unborn. His eyes hardened, as did his voice. "Tell me where you're staying and I'll drop you off and not bother you anymore."

"I will go no further with you."

"I just want to help you."

"I do not need your help." She shook free of his grip, took two steps down the road.

In one agile move, he stepped in front of her, blocking her way again. Containing a heavy sigh, she stopped short of plowing into him. Just short. They stood nearly nose to nose, close enough for her to see the beginnings of the stubble that would shadow his jaw in a few hours. Close enough for her to see the shadows in his eyes, too, though their source was less clear to her.

"Bull," he said.

She tilted her chin up. ''You are certainly acting like one.''

''Only because you're being unreasonable.''

''Because I don't wish to be *helped* by a man with my fiancé's blood on his hands?''

The ranger's face blanched, and at that moment she knew the source of the shadows in his eyes. Pain. Guilt. Shame. She would not have thought a *policía* capable of these emotions.

''You don't want my help?'' he said. ''Give me the number of someone to call for you. A name. Anything.''

''No.''

''No, you won't? Or no, you can't? There isn't anyone to call, is there? You have no one.''

Her face heated. ''That is none of your concern.''

''Lady, right now that is my *only* concern. Because until I know you have someone to go to, I'm stuck with you. And you're stuck with me.''

Sensing the turmoil in him, she could almost feel sorry for him. Almost, if the seedling sympathy sprouting inside her had not been quickly trampled by the stronger emotions she felt. Rage. Fear.

Hate.

She held on to the hate. It was the only emotion capable of keeping her on her feet. It gave her the strength to shoulder past him and start again down the blistering blacktop.

Behind her, his footfalls kept pace with her own. ''Eduardo's place has been sealed since the shooting. Where have you been staying?''

She ignored him.

''When was the last time you had a decent meal?'' he called to her.

At the mention of food, her knees nearly buckled. The

ranger's hands were on her shoulders, holding her, as she swayed. For a moment the broad male chest behind her was the only solid in a fluid world. The kick of his heart against her spine was a beacon, guiding her from the stormy sea to firm ground.

When the ground stopped rolling beneath her, he turned her gently toward him, the way a parent would nudge a tired child. Instinct screamed at her to resist, flee or fight, but she had the strength for neither. Unable to meet his gaze this time, she stared at his chest. Weakness was so uncharacteristic for her. Pregnancy was doing wild things to her body, her stamina. She hated the feeling of helplessness that consumed her.

"Please let me go," she said, humiliated by the pleading tone in her voice.

"Go where?" His words, like his hands, held her softly in place. "Back to San Ynez?"

Her gaze jumped to his, but before she could speak, he continued. "How do you plan on doing that with no plane ticket, no money, no credit cards? Nothing but your passport, some clothes, two bananas and a rosary to your name?"

She sucked in a sharp breath. "You searched my bag?"

"You left it in my car."

"And this gives you the right to invade my privacy?"

He scowled. She'd caught him, and she knew it. She had studied American culture enough to know they had laws about these things. Search and seizure. But since when had the *policía* in any country cared about the law?

"I thought you might have some medicine to settle your stomach," he said. "Or some crackers to nibble on."

"Inside my passport?"

He looked chagrined but defiant. "I was curious. It's not a crime."

"Is it a crime to force me to go with you when I have said I do not want your help?"

"I'm not going to let you just walk away. Not when you have nowhere to go."

Exasperation filled her voice. Had there ever before been such a stubborn man? "Where would you take me, Ranger?"

The question seemed to stump him for a moment, then he stammered, "I can help you get home."

The laugh that welled up inside her felt hysterical. "Do you know much about San Ynez?"

"Just that it's a small military dictatorship in South America."

"You are a Texas Ranger. An elite police officer. You must know more than that."

He drew his brows together. "It's rumored to be a major drug-producing nation, but it's still a poor country. All the money goes to the cartels, I suppose."

"It is a place where men are killed for resisting the military police who force them to manufacture narcotics. Women are given as rewards to the soldiers for their brutality and schools are closed so that the children may work in the coca fields. Yet this is the place you want to help me go back to?" Her hand curved protectively over her abdomen. "The place you would have me raise my child?"

"I just assumed—"

"You assumed wrong! I escaped San Ynez at the risk of my own death to give my child—Eduardo's child— the life it deserves. I will not go back." Her vehemence surprised her. Until now, she had assumed she would have to return to San Ynez, with Eduardo gone.

Poor Eduardo, who would never see his child.

Now, even considering going back to her homeland, to the violence, the madness of drugs, the death, made her stomach roll. She'd come to America for her child; she would stay for her child. Somehow.

The ranger's expression twisted as understanding set in. "You don't have residency in the U.S." Statement, not question.

"I am carrying the child of an American. That is all the residency I need."

He shook his head slowly. "I'm no immigration lawyer, but I don't think so. You'll be deported."

"Not if they can't find me." She angled her head, feeling superior now that she'd finally found an argument he couldn't counter. He was the police, bound by his law. He would not help her. She just hoped he wouldn't arrest her, either. "So, Ranger, do you still want to help me?"

He cocked his head to the side as he studied her for a long moment with intense eyes, then to her surprise, said seriously, "Yes. Yes, I do."

Del flexed his fingers on the steering wheel as he drove west, squinting into a sun so strong that tinted windows and aviator sunglasses both couldn't stop the glare. Elisa didn't seem to be bothered, though. She sat upright in the passenger seat, eyes forward and hands folded demurely in her lap. On the surface she looked harmless enough, even a little bit vulnerable, with the slight bulge in her midsection and the crinkles of worry at the corners of her eyes. Underneath, he suspected she was an entirely different woman. He sensed strength in her, more metaphysical than physical, and pride that could make her stubborn as a jackass.

Unfortunately, he also sensed she had good reason to be stubborn. He mentally sorted through the few facts he could recall about San Ynez, and the picture he put together wasn't pretty. The current government had taken power in a bloody coup and had quickly thrown an immature, but growing, nation into a state of economic infancy. Industry had been abandoned for the cultivation of narcotics; education ground to a halt; tourist attractions were converted into terrorist training facilities. All in the name of profit.

No wonder Elisa didn't want to go back.

She'd had a chance here, in the U.S.—a chance he'd taken away.

He glanced at her surreptitiously, found her almond complexion paled to alabaster and her expression frozen into a picture of complacency through what he figured had to be sheer willpower, as exhausted as she seemed to be.

Her gaze flicked toward him and he quickly looked away. Every time he caught a glimpse of her he found more to admire—her high, arching cheekbones, the dense brush of lashes over dark, feline eyes, the deep, wine color of her lips.

A horn blared close by. Too close. Looking toward the sound, Del realized his rearview mirror was just about scraping the side window of the pickup truck in the next lane. Adrenaline flooded his system in a hot surge. He jerked the steering wheel to the right, and the Land Rover lurched back to his half of the highway.

He'd been staring, he realized. And not at the road. The fight-or-flight instinct that had heated his blood cooled to lukewarm embarrassment. The driver of the pickup flipped a rude gesture at him, and Del waved pathetically in return.

At least Elisa hadn't noticed his lapse. She turned to him and blinked slowly, almost dazedly.

"Where are we going?" she asked.

Her *r*s rolled together in a sensual purr that pulled his own vocal chords tight as high wires. When was the last time he noticed anything about a woman other than whether or not her face matched one of the dozens of wanted flyers that crossed his desk each day?

He couldn't remember.

That bothered him. Maybe he'd gotten a little obsessive about his job. Lost perspective. But it bothered him even more that this woman was the one he chose to finally notice. A woman as out of reach to him as the moon to a howling coyote.

So where *was* he taking her?

Not to his place. Not when he couldn't keep his eyes off her. And not when he was under investigation for the death of her fiancé, for chrisakes. That kind of complication neither of them needed.

On the other hand, he couldn't just dump her at some cheap hotel alone. She needed clean clothes, a decent meal and maybe a little help from someone with some influence who would talk to the Immigration and Naturalization Service.

He blew out a sigh. She needed Gene Randolph.

Fifteen minutes later Del braked to a stop at the wrought-iron gate in front of the Randolph estate. When he lowered the window to punch the security code into the console, a small sound escaped the woman next to him. He hesitated, frowning at the deepening creases in her forehead. "You okay? You going to be sick again?"

"No," she said, breathlessly, and he wasn't sure if she meant no, she was not okay, or no, she was not going to be sick again.

"This is your home?" she asked.

He glanced at the sprawling grounds beyond the gate. An automatic irrigation system kept the lawn emerald green even in the most arid conditions. Grand oaks shaded the path to the house, surrounded by flowering crepe myrtle in red, pink and white, beds of Mexican heather and trellises covered with climbing yellow roses in full bloom. "No." Not on a ranger's salary. "It belongs to a friend."

Her hand trembled on the door handle. He frowned.

"This is the Randolph estate," he explained. "Gene Randolph, maybe you heard of him? Two-term governor of Texas a while back."

"Diós," she muttered. *"Un político."*

She clutched her tattered olive bag with her left hand and made the sign of the cross with the right. When she turned to him, all hints of dazedness had vanished from her eyes, replaced by sharp, clear fear. "Please let me go. I cannot stay here."

Chapter 3

"You got something against politicians?" Del asked. The words sounded casual, but the look that accompanied them made Elisa's stomach churn. This time the illness had little to do with her pregnancy.

She was defenseless against that sharp, gray gaze of his. It pierced the armor of aloofness in which she'd cloaked herself, like a knife through an overripe mango. The ranger's eyes cut to the core of her. Bared her very essence. Given enough time, all her secrets would be exposed to him. All her doubts.

She couldn't let that happen. She'd lived in the jungle long enough to know better than to show weakness to a predator.

"Politicians are all corrupt." Even to her own ears, her voice sounded venomous. Lifting her chin, she turned away. The wrought-iron gate before them clanked and swung open with a mechanical buzz. Past it, park-like grounds rolled over a series of low hills. A red-brick mansion lorded over the estate from the highest knoll. Three stories high and Georgian in style, with thick white pillars supporting wide, shady porches hung with green ferns on all three levels, the house looked big enough to sleep an army. A wing swept back from each side of the stacked porches. Elisa counted seven windows she assumed to be bedrooms on each floor of each wing.

Make that two armies.

Her chest burned with the fire of the oppressed. How many slept in gutters so that one man could sleep in opulence?

"All those who live like this are criminals, or they take kickbacks to let the criminals operate. Like cannibals, they feed off of their own people," she added.

Despite the danger to her privacy, Elisa turned back to him, ready to meet the sharp point of his gaze. To her surprise, she found him staring out the windshield as if trying to see the landscape through her eyes.

"Not Gene Randolph," he finally said, shaking his head. Whatever he'd been looking for, he hadn't found it.

Elisa hadn't expected him to. He couldn't possibly see what she saw. He hadn't lived her hell. Had never been dragged through a place like the house on the hill, as she had. Marched through the dining hall where guests ate off bone china, to the cellar where she ate with the rats.

The memory brought a cold sweat to the back of her neck. She smelled fear and the stink of human excrement, heard the cries of the dying, as if she were back in that hole. Instinctively her hand covered her abdomen protectively.

"He's a good man," the ranger said. Behind them the

gate clanked shut, sounding to Elisa's ears like a cell door. "You can trust him."

A disbelieving laugh bubbled up within her. "You want me to trust a politician?" She rolled her gaze toward him. "Ranger, I do not even trust *you.*"

He didn't say anything, but his lips seemed thinner as he put the car in gear and eased it forward. The silver glow in his eyes dimmed. If she didn't know better, she'd think he was…hurt?

Because she didn't trust him?

He had made a good show so far of playing the repentant warrior, bound by honor to help the woman left behind by the man he had killed in error. But surely he did not expect her to put her faith, her *fate* and that of her baby, in his hands so easily. He couldn't possibly. And still her lack of trust bothered him.

His reaction confused her. Where she came from, men like him—*policía*—didn't care what people like her thought. She was no one to him. Yet he had not treated her like no one. Another day, another time, she would have liked to ask why. Today, here, she just wanted to get away, to grieve for Eduardo and raise her child alone.

She had found a way to escape a place like this once before. She would find a way again. Soon.

"This Randolph, he is in charge of the Texas Rangers?" she asked, fingering the door handle nervously.

"No, we have a new governor now." He didn't look at her.

"Then why have we come here?"

"Because Gene knows how the system works. And he still has a lot of influence."

Influence. A fancy word for power. Control. The ability to crush lives. People. Elisa's pulse fluttered in the base of her throat like a fledgling's wings.

"He doesn't even know me. Why would he use his...*influence* to help me?"

"Because he does know me. And Gene stands by his friends."

The ranger still did not look at her. She thought he was still insulted that she doubted his motivations, and now she had questioned his friend's honor, too. It occurred to her that provoking him further might not be wise. Antagonizing him would only make escape more difficult.

Carefully she blunted the edge of her uneasiness until she could speak in what she hoped would sound like a conversational tone. "You and this politician are close?"

He nodded, a measure of the tension slipping from his expression. "I guess you could say that. I've known Gene since my highway patrol days. I, ah, helped him out of a jam once."

He rubbed his thigh absently as if it ached. Elisa recognized the gesture. She saw it too often in her country, the soothing of phantom pain from an old wound.

"Gene kind of took me under his wing after that. Helped me get into the Rangers. Even put me up here in town. My family has a farm about ninety miles north of here. It was getting to be a hell of a commute." He nodded down a lane that cut off the main driveway toward a two-story structure that replicated the architecture, if not the size, of the main house. "Guess I just never got around to moving out. I stay in the apartment above the carriage house there."

"So he owes you."

"No," the ranger said quickly. Too quickly. Then he shrugged. "Maybe he feels like he does. But he shouldn't. I was just doing my job."

"Your job required you to take a bullet for him?"

His jaw slanted sideways. "How did you know?"

"Now he provides you a place to live."

His forehead creased. "It's not some kind of kickback, if that's what you mean. I pay rent."

"Even better."

"What is that supposed to mean?"

She'd vowed not to antagonize him, but she couldn't help herself. Politicians were the same worldwide, it seemed. "He is a rich man. Rich men have enemies, no? People who would hurt them for their money."

"I suppose."

"So for nothing more than the use of his garage, your friend takes your money every month, *and* gets a Texas Ranger guarding his front door." A smug smile slipped over her lips as she shook her head. *"Políticos."*

"Gene isn't using me, if that's what you're thinking."

She studied the flowering crepe myrtle lining the driveway. The ranger sighed noisily.

"Maybe having a cop close by makes him more comfortable," he said. "If so, I'm glad to give him the peace of mind."

She turned toward him. "Because he was your governor?"

"Because he is my friend." He enunciated each word quietly, but with vehemence. She looked away. Did he really think she would so easily accept that he was exactly what he seemed, an honorable man, helping her in an effort to right the wrong he had done, and his friend, a politician, would help without a hidden agenda or profit motive?

No, he could not. *She* could not. Yet as the car came to a stop in the paved circle outside the mansion and the ranger lead her to the front door, she wanted to believe it.

But she had survived eight years of civil war in her country by being cautious, by relying on herself and trusting precious few. The cloak of vigilance she had sheathed herself in was hard to shed. Especially after what had happened to Eduardo.

Coming to America was to have been her chance to escape violence. She had not planned the baby she and Eduardo had created, but once she'd learned of it and accepted his offer of marriage in the United States, she had dreamed of a better life. She had dreamed of a quiet little apartment and nights filled with the sounds of city life—traffic and music and laughing voices on the street—instead of mortar fire and the cries of the dying.

She had dreamed of peace.

When she arrived in America and saw the father of her child gunned down, she had realized the idyllic life she sought did not exist.

Like all dreams, peace was only an illusion.

A trick of the mind.

Del cruised up the winding drive toward the Randolph mansion slower than was necessary to buy time to think. Gene would expect an explanation when Del showed up at his door with Elisa in tow. The problem was, there weren't any explanations. None that made sense. Del was under investigation for the death of this woman's fiancé. Every moment he spent in her company further compromised his position. Helping her could cast doubt on his motivations. Raise questions about his character. The cautious thing to do would be to keep as far away from her as possible.

But then, caution had never been high on his list of priorities. He wouldn't have become a Texas Ranger if it had been. In his world, a person had two choices in every situation: he could do the right thing or the wrong thing. An honorable man always did the right thing, even if it wasn't the safe choice or the obvious one. Helping Elisa Reyes definitely wasn't safe. The press would come down on him like a bobcat on a wounded bird if they found out, but leaving her, pregnant and alone, to make her own way wasn't a decision he could live with. Not when he was responsible for putting her in this situation.

None of that would make explaining her presence to Gene Randolph any easier. With his silvering hair and perpetually paternal expression, Gene might look like everybody's grandfather, but he was sharp as a straight razor. One look at the edge in his pale-blue eyes when the door opened told Del that introductions wouldn't be necessary. Gene knew exactly who Elisa was. What he didn't know was what the hell she was doing on his doorstep with Del.

They made small talk as they crossed the black-and-white marble-tiled foyer, and two minutes later were settled into Gene's library/office. Bookcases rose from the floor to the ceiling behind Gene's massive mahogany desk. Law books, mostly, lined the shelves, but the spines of those on the lower racks sported popular fiction titles, mysteries and novelized true war stories. The fact that these were within easiest reach of Gene's oversize leather chair reflected his friend's retired status, Del figured.

For a moment he regretted dragging his friend back into the bureaucratic world he'd escaped. If anyone deserved his peace, it was Gene. But twenty years in politics had given the former governor a way with sticky situations, and Del's predicament was about as sticky as a fresh roll of flypaper.

"What do you know about alien residency requirements?'' Del asked, ending the small talk. Propping his elbows on his knees, he leaned forward in his wing chair. In the matching seat next to him, Elisa sat back, her ankles and knees pressed together and her hands in her lap.

''You don't sit in the governor's chair in Texas without going around the block a few times with the INS.'' Raising his sterling eyebrows gently, Gene studied them both across the desk. ''I take it Ms. Reyes is the alien in question?''

Del didn't consider it was his place to talk about Elisa's situation, so he waited for her to explain. A heartbeat passed, then another, before she inclined her head stiffly. Silently.

Damn the woman's pride. It would be her undoing.

''I understand you were engaged to Eduardo Garcia,'' Gene said softly.

Again she simply nodded, ending with her chin high. She looked noble, genteel, bearing her fate with the serenity of a Madonna. And beneath it all, despite her best attempts to cover it up, she looked sad.

''I'm sorry,'' Gene said, meeting her gaze head-on and holding it. If Del wasn't mistaken, his simple sincerity earned him a notch of respect from Elisa.

''You are not at fault,'' she said.

Del felt the disclaimer like a kick in the gut. They all knew who shouldered the blame for this situation.

''We need to know how to get her green card even now that Eduardo is... Even without Eduardo,'' he said, forcing his jaw to release its clench.

Gene's eyelids drooped sadly as he broke eye contact with Elisa and looked at Del. ''If the marriage never took place—''

''There's got to be some way,'' Del said.

Gene thought. "Do you have a marriage license? Any documentation?"

Elisa hesitated only a second before shaking her head.

"Then I'm afraid there's nothing—"

"She's pregnant," Del cut in harshly. "It's Garcia's baby. An American baby."

"Not until it's born, it's not," Gene said gently. "And not without Garcia around to acknowledge it as his. There's no way to prove—"

Del shoved to his feet, rocking his chair. "Are you saying she's lying?"

He surprised himself with his fervor. Who was he to leap to her defense? He was not exactly her knight in shining armor.

Gene warned him off with narrowed eyes. "I'm saying that the INS will not document this baby as an American citizen without proof. Proof we don't appear to have."

"We'll do a DNA test."

"Four or five months from now, when the baby is born, maybe. But Ms. Reyes will have been deported by then, most likely. Even if you find facilities in San Ynez to run their end of the procedure, you're going to need Garcia's DNA to match to. The exhumation order alone could take months. Then after the matching, there's INS applications, interviews—"

"Are you telling me it's hopeless?" Stalking across the room he rubbed the knotted muscles in the back of his neck. "There's got to be a way to keep her here."

"I didn't say it was hopeless," Gene said. "Just that it wouldn't be easy."

He raised his head. "So where do we start?"

Gene focused on Elisa. "With a soft bed and a hot meal."

Elisa's eyes widened.

Gene turned to Del and said, "Ms. Reyes looks like she could use some rest. Why don't you show her upstairs to one of the guest rooms while I go see what I can wrangle up in the kitchen? Tomorrow I'll make some calls, see what I can find out."

One look at Elisa and Del realized Gene was right. She sat with her back straight and her shoulders square, but her almond complexion had paled to chalk and her neck was corded with strain. Blue circles dragged her eyelids down. She looked like a woman holding on to her dignity by her last fingernail.

She didn't want her fate in the hands of politician; she'd made that clear before they'd arrived. But there was nothing more to do tonight. Del doubted she'd be happy about staying with Gene, but she couldn't stay with him. There was a line between honor and insanity, and taking a beautiful, vulnerable, untouchable woman to his tiny apartment definitely fell on the crazy side.

Gene's offer was generous. This was the best place for her. The only place for her, he told himself as he led her into a room decorated in peonies and lace and smelling like water lilies. At least every time she looked at Gene through those fathomless dark-chocolate eyes of hers, she wouldn't be looking at the man who ruined her life.

So why, as he said his goodbyes and closed the door on the fear she tried—unsuccessfully—to hide from him, did he feel as if he was abandoning her?

The room belonged on the pages of a storybook. Elisa stood in the center and turned a slow circle, taking it all in. Ruffles exploded from every seam of the comforter covering the huge four-poster bed. The gauzy canopy over it matched the drapes filtering the sunset through the window. The water pitcher on the cherry wood dresser looked antique, and the carpet underfoot was as thick and soft as the moss floor of a rainforest.

She sat on the edge of the bed and ran her hand over the cover. As a child she'd dreamed of having a room like this. She'd played make-believe and pretended her cot was a mattress as soft as a lamb, like this one, and that sheets full of fresh-smelling flowers like these surrounded her while she slept. But she wasn't a child anymore. In a few months she would have a baby of her own to care for.

Randolph had said she would be deported. She couldn't let that happen. Her baby didn't have a chance in San Ynez.

She had to leave tonight. *La Migra* couldn't deport her if they couldn't find her. She didn't know what kind of life she and her child would have here, but it had to be better than the certain death that awaited in her country.

She lay down on her side, her knees drawn up and her palm spread on her belly. Downstairs she heard voices still. The ranger and the politician. She would have to wait until the house was quiet to make her escape. Until then she would rest. She was tired. So tired…

She closed her eyes. With the sound of his voice drifting up to her, his image formed in her mind. They both stood on clouds of lace and ruffles in a soft, beautiful place. But a great wind kicked up, buffeted them, and then she was falling, falling and beneath her the ranger waited, his strong arms open, ready to catch her.

"Everyone's looking for a fall guy, Coop. And you're the most likely candidate. Getting mixed up with her isn't going to help your case."

Leaning his hips against Gene's kitchen counter, Del folded his arms over his chest and scowled. "What am I supposed to do, let her be sent back to that hell hole she came from?"

"I'm not sure you're going to have much choice." Del's scowl deepened. "Hold on, now," Gene said, raising his hand. "I didn't say we couldn't work on it. But face it, in the end, you may have to let her go."

The possibility left a hole the size of the Grand Canyon in Del's chest. He wasn't ready to face it yet. Wasn't sure what he would do if it came down to it. He wasn't just trying to save Elisa Reyes, he realized. He was trying to save himself. From a long, slow death by guilt. "What do you know about the investigation?" he asked to change the subject.

"Not much."

Del snorted. "When you ask questions, people answer. And I know you've been asking questions. You've got to know something."

"Nothing I should be telling you."

"Come on, Gene. You're not going to stonewall me, too, are you? I just want to know what's going on."

The creases in Gene's face deepened. He aged a decade in the span of seconds. "They've got one dead gun dealer and one dead security guard. Nothing to suggest it's not exactly what it looks like. An innocent man caught in the crossfire."

"They verified his employment, that he was supposed to be working that day?"

"Ten minutes after the shooting."

"And he's not in any our of the databases, NCIC, Interpol? No ties to smuggling, gangs, drugs, any of the usual suspects?" If it could be proven that Eduardo Garcia had somehow been part of the gun deal gone bad, it would mean that he'd willingly put himself in harm's way for the purpose of criminal activity. In the eyes of the law, he, then, not Del, was liable for his death. The investigators would declare it a good shoot.

Del would be vindicated. Not that it would make him feel any better.

Gene shook his head, deflating Del's hope. "He's so clean he squeaks."

Desperation left Del's throat raw. "What about the two that got away? Maybe they know something."

"No sign of them. What about the woman? What did you get out of her? She know anything?"

Del's head snapped up, eyes narrowed. "Is that why you think I brought her here? To find out what she knows?"

"She didn't tell the DPS guys much. It occurred to me you could help your case if you got her to talk."

Del cursed, loudly and violently, before yanking the back door open and stepping out. Gene caught it just before it slammed shut behind him. He chuckled. "Calm down, boy. I didn't mean anything."

When Del turned, Gene stood on the stoop with his hands in his pockets like a recalcitrant teen. "The hell you didn't," Del accused.

"All right, so maybe I just wanted to hear you deny it myself." He took a step into the grass. "And if I question your motivations, you know others are going to. You're taking a big risk hooking up with her."

"What was I supposed to do, leave her lying on the side of the highway?"

"No, don't suppose you could have done that." Hands still in his pockets, Gene rocked heel to toe, waiting.

Del turned his head up to the sky. The stars were

coming out on another perfectly clear Texas night. "It's my fault, Gene."

"And now you gotta fix it."

"Yeah, if I can."

"You can't save them all, Del."

Del didn't want to think about that, not here, not now. *No, but I can damn sure try to save this one.*

But that thought pealed through his mind like church bells all the way back to the carriage house. In his apartment he couldn't concentrate on the book he'd been reading for the maelstrom in his head. He couldn't unwind, so he made himself a cup of decaf coffee and went out to sit on the back stairs to the apartment. Usually he found the view calming. He could see all the way to downtown Dallas. Watch the big lighted ball on top of Reunion Tower turn.

He could see that all was right with his corner of the world.

Only, tonight nothing felt right.

What if he couldn't save her?

No. He refused to think that way. He couldn't bring Garcia back to life. Maybe he couldn't even repair the damage to his career or fill this great, yawning emptiness inside him. But he could damn well keep Elisa Reyes in the United States where she and her child would be safe.

He stopped, the surety of that one thought gusting through him like a gale-force wind. Whatever it took, he could not let Elisa Reyes be sent back to San Ynez. Whether she wanted his help or not, she would have it. He owed her that much.

And Del Cooper damn well paid his debts.

Elisa hadn't meant to fall asleep, but she'd been so tired. The men's voices—the politician and the policeman—had droned on. She'd listened, but her eyelids had grown heavy.

Now the night, and her chance to escape, was almost over. According to the clock by the bed, dawn would break in another hour, and she panicked as she remembered last night's conversations.

She couldn't go back to San Ynez. She wouldn't let them send her.

Anger and fear razed her nerves, making her hands shake. She'd come to America to start a new life for her child. Eduardo was gone, but he would want her to stay, to give their child that life even without him. How could a parent not want that?

Silently Elisa rose and found her boots, her bag. She'd seen two cars in the garage the ranger called the carriage house last night. It didn't take long for her to find the keys hung neatly in a cabinet by the door. Apparently the politician counted on the iron gate around his property and the ranger who lived above his precious cars to protect them. The lock on that cabinet wouldn't stop anyone.

Inside the convertible with the leaping jaguar on the hood, she fumbled with the keyring. Quietly. She had to be quiet, or the ranger would hear.

Pushing the only key she hadn't yet tried into the ignition, she dropped the whole ring. *Ay, Diós.* Then she crossed herself for her transgression. When she bent her head to retrieve the keys, the seat creaked beneath her. The rich smell of leather filled her senses as she groped around the floorboard.

When she finally got a grip on the keys and raised her head, she found the ranger standing just beyond the front bumper. His thick forearms were folded over his broad chest, and the starlight behind him gave his gray eyes a silvery glow, pinning her in place.

"Going somewhere?" he asked.

Breaking the eye contact, she shoved the key home and twisted. The engine purred to life. Before she could put it in gear, though, the car dipped and jounced. She jerked her head up. Her eyes widened at the sight of the ranger's boots clomping across the polished hood. He easily hopped over the windshield and landed in the seat next to her. "Don't mind if I tag along, do you?" he asked. "Just to make sure Gene gets his car back."

She flinched at the implication that she was stealing the car. Of course, she *was* stealing the car. But it was necessary. Her child's life was at stake. "Let me go," she said, angling her chin.

Casually he reached over and switched off the ignition. "I can't do that."

"Why? What do you want from me?"

"Nothing. Except to help you."

"So that you can clear your conscience?"

His eyes turned cold. "Lady, it's going to take a lot more than you to clear my conscience."

"Then let me go."

"Go where? San Ynez?"

Her anger flared to match his. Her hands clenched around the steering wheel. "No. I can't go back there." Going home meant certain death. She couldn't escape the soldiers with a baby.

"Where, then?"

"I will find a place." She could take care of herself. She'd been taking care of herself—and a lot of other people—for eight years now.

"On the street? What kind of life is that?"

"Is it worse than starving in San Ynez? Being hunted

by military police who protect the coca fields and massacre their own people?'' She forced herself to take a deep breath. ''I will survive.''

''And your baby?''

Elisa's cramped stomach muscles fluttered, reminding her of the child within. She could take care of herself, she was sure of that. But a baby? She could stitch an open wound with a sewing needle, defuse an antipersonnel land mine with a screwdriver and a stick. But she knew nothing about babies. Delivering them or caring for them.

He had a way of striking at the core of her fears, this ranger.

''At least he will have a chance,'' she said, laying her hand protectively over her middle. Del followed the movement with his eyes, his lips tightening.

''There is another way. For both of you.''

She didn't want to ask how. Wouldn't trust him even when he answered, despite that dependable-looking face and the sincerity in his expression. But how could she keep silent with all she had at stake? ''What way?''

''There are immigration lawyers. They can appeal your case to the INS.''

''So that *La Migra* knows right where to find me when they're ready to throw me out? No.''

''Gene Randolph has contacts in the State Department. He might be able to push something through. A hardship application or political asylum.''

Elisa laughed in disbelief. ''Put my fate in the hands of Immigration *and* a politician?''

''Give the system a chance. No one wants you to suffer because of what happened to Eduardo.''

To her horror, her eyes suddenly warmed, watered. Despising the weakness, and blaming it on hormones, she blinked back the tears. "I trusted the system once, in my country," she said, when she was sure her voice wouldn't shake. "I went to the university and studied economics and English. I worked within our government to build industry and commerce. I spoke to student groups about making our country stronger, improving trade relations with America and Europe. I was giving this speech when a colonel in the army of San Ynez, Colonel Sanchez, decided he should run the country, not the elected president. With the troops behind him, he overran the presidential palace. Presidente Herrerra was taken to sea and killed, and Sanchez became our new leader. I was thrown in jail, chained and interrogated as a dissident for three days before I escaped with my brothers. So forgive me if I do not easily trust the system."

She expected the ranger to be shocked, then to argue that that was San Ynez. This was America. The great, infallible America.

He surprised her. His expression warmed, not with anger, but with understanding. His mouth almost smiled, as if a weight had been lifted from the corners with the making of some great decision. He covered her hand on the steering wheel with his, lifted it, held her fingers lightly. His hands weren't smooth; she knew that from other times he'd touched her. But for the first time, she realized she liked their coarseness. Roughened hands were a sign of strength. A symbol of a man's dedication to a cause, be it chopping wood or plowing fields. She wondered how Ranger Cooper had earned his calluses.

"Okay then, don't trust the system," he said, his voice a smooth contrast to his rough hands. "Just trust me."

She stared at him, unsure what to say next. She couldn't trust him. He was *policía*—the worst of the worst in her country. But something about him tugged at her, made her want to believe. Perhaps just her emotions, run away again.

"I've been doing a lot of thinking the last few hours, and there is one sure way to guarantee you can stay in America."

"Eduardo was the only way." Her voice sounded faraway, small.

"No," he said. He paused. When she brought her eyes back to his, his chest rose and fell with a single deep breath before he spoke. "You can marry me instead."

Chapter 4

"*¿Estas loco?* I cannot marry you!"

Elisa jerked her hand from the ranger's. The soft scrape of his callused palm on her fingertips shot a tingle of awareness up her arm. Or maybe that was just shock. A physical reaction to an emotional jolt.

Marry him? He could not be serious.

But one look at his pewter eyes, glowing in the dim light, convinced her that he was serious. Deadly so. He did not just stare at her. He focused his entire being on her. He looked at her as though the rest of the world had faded away, as if nothing else existed except him and her and the moonlight and the ridiculously expensive car in which they sat.

The supple leather seat groaned as she scrambled away. Pulling her feet onto the seat, she jammed her back into the corner between the passenger seat and door and drew her knees to her chest. Even at this distance, the ranger was too close, too sincere and much too intense.

"It wouldn't be a real marriage," he explained as calmly as if he were showing her how to use a blender. "I mean…it would have to be legal. But it would just be a piece of paper between us. It wouldn't mean anything. Not really."

She knew he was talking about…intimate relations, and decided not to respond to that implication. Sex with the ranger was the last of her worries. Too outrageous to ponder. "It would mean a great deal. It would mean I would be bound to you. Dependent on you."

"Only for two years. After that the INS considers you a resident regardless of your marital status. You can divorce me and stay in the States. Legally."

Elisa gulped in a breath. She could not spend two years with him. She could not spend two minutes with him without her pulse dipping and jumping like a monkey swinging through the trees.

"Why?" she asked. Her breath came out like a whisper. "Why would you do this?"

He closed his eyes a moment, and the light played off the broad brush of his eyelashes. When he looked at her again, the metallic glimmer of his irises had dimmed. Tarnished.

"I can't give back the things I took from you—the husband you deserve and a father for your child. But I can give you a home here, in the United States. A safe place where your baby can get an education. See a doctor. Live." He swallowed. When he spoke again his voice was deeper. Rougher. "I can't give you back the love you lost, or happiness. But I can give you security. I can give you peace."

Peace. The illusion again. The dream.

A cold knot of anger hardened inside her. "I'll take nothing from you. Not even peace." She fumbled for the door latch, determined to get away.

Quick as lightning his hand flashed out, captured her wrist. "Because you hate me that much? Or because you're too proud to admit that you need help?"

She pulled once, experimentally, on her arm, but found the circle of fingers around her wrist as inescapable as the coil of a hungry boa constrictor around its prey. "It is not pride that causes my mistrust, Ranger, but self-preservation. You are *policía*."

"I am a man trying to do the right thing."

"And I am a woman trying to save my child. I cannot accept your help."

"Because I'm a cop?"

"Because you killed Eduardo."

"I didn't know he was there." His voice rasped like a dull saw on hardwood.

"Tell me, Ranger. If I claimed I did not know the speed limit on the road outside was thirty-five miles per hour, and you found me going sixty, would you still write me a ticket?"

The ranger's eyes narrowed. Not in a glare, but as if he were in pain. "I made a mistake. But I'm trying to make up for it now. I won't hurt you."

She looked pointedly at the hold he still had on her arm. Her fingers were beginning to tingle from the lack of blood. "You are hurting me now."

His gaze dropped guiltily to where his broad hand circled her wrist an instant before his fingers uncoiled with the force of a broken spring. Shouldering the car door open behind her, Elisa left him without looking back.

She made it halfway down the winding drive before she heard footsteps behind her. The ranger paced her, making no attempt to catch up, but not letting her go, either.

She hurried her gait. Gooseflesh prickled her skin, but not from fear. The ranger wouldn't hurt her, not physically. She wasn't sure when she'd come to believe that, but she knew it now. Felt it soul deep.

The danger he posed to her was emotional. He threatened her sense of self-reliance. He exposed her weaknesses.

For years she'd taken care of herself and many others. She could take care of herself now. Herself and a baby.

At the entrance to the Randolph estate, she grabbed the iron gate, rattling it angrily when it refused to yield.

The ranger stepped up behind her, close enough she could feel his moist body heat mingle with the dry heat of the night. "It's secured. Won't open without a code."

A code he had, but would not share, no doubt.

Panic rose up in her throat. She was a prisoner here, as she had once been in San Ynez. Glancing up, she hooked a foot on the lowest bar and started climbing.

"Hey, hey!" he said behind her, a moment before one thick arm encircled her waist. "What do you think you're doing?"

"Leaving," she said kicking her legs futilely as he pulled her off the fence. Her blouse was hooked on a wrought iron prong. When he reached to free it she landed a solid blow on his thigh.

He winced, tightening his grip on her waist and capturing her flailing legs between his thighs. "Let me help you, God damn it."

Weakly she crossed herself, automatically muttering an appeal for his forgiveness for the transgression of cursing. Her shirt ripped free of the fence, exposing the rise of one breast. The ranger stumbled backward, still holding her.

"You want to help me, Ranger?" she cried. "Help me escape."

He spit a strand of her hair out of his mouth and set her on her feet, turning her toward him. "So that you can pick cotton in the sun all day with a baby strapped to your back? Or scrub someone else's floors on your hands and knees and pick up some rich kid's hundred-dollar toys while your kid plays with a stick in the dirt? Because those are the realities of life for a female illegal alien in this country. And that's if you can find work at all. Work that doesn't require you to be flat on your back, that is."

He spoke quickly, and she struggled to keep up with his meaning. By the time she realized what he'd implied, his gaze was brushing up and down her length with the weight, and heat, of a physical touch. Suppressing the tremor his imaginary caress provoked, she pulled out of his grasp and willed her rubbery legs to hold her. The short struggle had robbed her of her strength.

"You're pretty," he said, his voice softening, almost cooing. "You'll do all right at first. But that kind of work has a way of taking a toll on a girl. Ages her. How long do you think it will be before you're turning twenty-dollar tricks in the cab of some redneck's pickup to pay for baby food?"

Elisa put every bit of the strength she had left into her swing. He raised his forearm, blocking her fist an inch from his cheek, but momentum carried her body forward. She crashed into his chest with an audible grunt.

He held her there, not tightly as a prisoner, but supporting. Steadying her cheek against his shoulder.

She lacked the strength to pull away, and suspected he knew it. "Bastard," she breathed against his hot skin.

An amused smile pulled at one corner of his mouth. "I thought you didn't swear."

"I do not take the Lord's name in vain."

He eased her away. She swayed, but managed to stand. "Good for you," he said. "My grandmother is going to love you."

"I have no intention of meeting your grandmother."

"You don't have the strength to walk, much less run away. Maybe it's time to rethink this escape plan of yours."

He was right, not that she would admit it out loud. She was in no shape to strike out on her own, penniless and friendless in a foreign land.

That didn't mean she was going to marry him.

It did, however, require her to swallow some of her pride. Maybe if she let him help her in some other way, he would leave her alone and forget this crazy marriage idea.

Gazing up at the determined lines of his face, she licked her lips. "Perhaps you could help me. I need to purchase transportation and pay for food and lodging until I can—"

His lip curled. "You won't marry me, but you'll take my money? What is Eduardo's death worth to you? Ten thousand dollars? Twenty?"

Tears of shame pooled in Elisa's eyes. She closed her fist again, but could not muster the strength to lift it. Instead she turned and rattled the gate. A feral cry rose in her throat when it still refused to open. She went wild then, kicking the heavy iron and pounding the bars until one of her knuckles split. She lifted one foot to climb and felt herself lifted from behind, gently turned.

She lashed out as violently at the man who held her as she had at the gate that imprisoned her. Her hair whipped around her face like the limbs of a sapling in a tropical storm. Her cry became a keen, then a wail.

He held her to him gently, cupping her head and back, but letting her arms and legs fly free. Letting her strike and pound and kick. When her strength waned and she was reduced to tangling her fists in his shirt and tugging, he lifted her into his arms and carried her back to the carriage house.

Exhaustion claimed her before he reached the door, but when he tucked her into a wide bed with a tartan plaid comforter, she roused enough to see that her catharsis had drained him as much as her. All the color had leached from his face, and his eyes were as pale as white gold. He looked empty inside, his energy, his life force gone. Even his voice sounded hollow when he spoke.

"I'll pull together all the cash I can get my hands on." His fingers were cool when they pushed a strand of hair from her cheek. "As soon as the banks open Monday."

The bells at St. Thomas, the Catholic church down the road, had yet to announce the 9:00-a.m. mass and already the thermometer in Del's garden read a hundred degrees. Carefully pushing aside a thorny limb in the bed of yellow roses that lined the south side of the carriage house, he lifted a trowelful of soil from around the roots of the largest bush and shook a tangle of earthworms from the jar he held into the shallow hole. He smiled as the critters burrowed deeper into the earth. According to Pete Miller at Miller's Feed and Seed, the worms would aerate the soil and Del would have roses blooming until Christmas this year.

As he gently evened out the loose dirt, a shadow fell over him. He had to give the woman credit. She could move without making a sound. Not many people could sneak up on a Texas Ranger.

"You are a gardener."

He shrugged without turning. "I putter."

"I would think Mr. Randolph would pay someone to tend his plants."

"He does. Around his house. But the carriage house is my home. I take care of what's mine."

Just as he would take care of her, if she would let him.

Wiping his forehead with the back of his hand, he bit back last night's bitterness. Today was a new day, and he had new plans.

He troweled up a new clod of dirt, shook out a few more worms. "How are you feeling?"

"You mean, am I going to go *loco* and attack you again?"

"No. I mean *how are you feeling?*" Meticulously, he checked the leaves of the rosebush for black spot. The rich scent of mulch mingled with the sweet smell of the roses and something sharper. Soap and shampoo. Vanilla and almond. Her unique female scent.

"I am…better."

"You want to talk about what happened last night?"

"No."

Good. He wasn't sure he wanted to talk about it, either. Talking wasn't his strongest suit. Especially talking about a fit of rage so strong it nearly turned a willful, prideful woman into a raving banshee.

She'd scared the hell out of him last night and made him realize he couldn't force his will on her, not without breaking her, and he couldn't bear to see such spirit crushed. From now on he planned a more subtle approach.

"Where are my clothes?" she asked, changing the subject smoothly.

"In the dryer. If you didn't hear them tumbling, then they're probably done."

"Thank you for the loan of something clean."

Well that was a change. A truce? He turned to ask, and found the woman was right behind him. How she'd gotten there without him hearing her move, he couldn't guess. He shifted so that he could see her.

She stood before him in a pair of gray sweatpants with six extra inches of length billowing around her ankles and a Dallas Cowboys football jersey so large that the neck hole spilled over one shoulder. He'd left the shirt out for her because it was cropped at the midriff. He hoped it wouldn't swallow her.

He'd been right. And he'd been very, very wrong. The midriff shirt hung to her waist, leaving her delicate navel exposed and highlighting the way the sagging sweats barely clung to the swell of her hips.

Del's mouth dried up as if she was standing there in a scrap of black lace. He forced his gaze up to hers.

Her eyes widened, pinpointed on the side of his neck. "Did I do that?"

His hand automatically raised to the raw, stinging furrow her fingernail had left in him last night. "I don't think you were aiming for me, if it's any consolation."

"It's not." Her hand raised next to his, hovered a second and then traced a path just below the wound.

Inexplicably, the pulse in Del's jugular jumped to meet her fingertips.

"I am sorry," she said, running her fingers back the

way they had come and brushing the underside of his jaw with her knuckles.

He wasn't. God help him, but if it took the sharp point of hatred out of her eyes when she looked at him, if it allowed her to touch him like that, light and stirring, he wasn't sorry a bit. The pulse in other places besides his jugular leaped.

Realizing he was reading more into her touch than she'd meant by it, he took a step back—right into the rosebush.

"Ouch! Sh—" He bit back the rest of the curse, grabbing the thorny branch before it attached itself to any more of his anatomy. By the time he'd detached the bush from the seat of his jeans and turned back to Elisa, she had her lower lip pulled between her teeth. One giggle escaped as he stood gaping at her, then another.

He rubbed his backside, and she laughed outright. The sound was like champagne—full of sparkles and bubbles and potent enough to get a man drunk just listening to it.

Then the nine-o'clock bells called the faithful to service at St. Thomas, and the moment ended as unexpectedly as it had begun.

A new wall of guilt crashed down on Del. He felt as if God spoke to him through the bells. He had no right enjoying Elisa's laugh, much less her touch or the way she looked in his old clothes. She was another man's woman.

At least she had been.

Elisa cocked her head, listening to the deep, chiming melody with her fingertips pressed to her pursed lips. When the bells quieted she asked, her eyes hopeful, "There is a church near here?"

He nodded, regret burning the back of his throat. "Half mile down the road."

"I would like to go."

He angled his head in capitulation. "Sure."

He couldn't sit with her, couldn't risk being seen with her, but he could drop her off, circle around and sneak into a back pew where he could keep an eye on her.

It had been a long time since he'd bent a knee in prayer. Maybe it would do him good.

He had a lot to ask forgiveness for.

"This does not look like a bank," Elisa said, twisting in her seat to peer at the four-story white granite building Del had pulled up to.

"Isn't."

She frowned. "Then why have we stopped here?" Yesterday, after church, he'd taken her shopping and bought more than she needed—more than she had ever owned—to take with her when she left. At his insistence, she had picked out two summer shirts, matching shorts with soft elastic waists and a shift dress that would accommodate her expanding midsection for some time. To her surprise he'd added a bathrobe, a baggy sweatsuit, a pair of knit pants, two blouses and sneakers along with a wide assortment of toiletries and underwear.

Surely she couldn't need anything else.

He wiped his palm over his left thigh, a sign she'd learned meant she wouldn't like what came next. "I made you a doctor's appointment. Figured you'd want to make sure everything's all right with the baby before you took off."

Her palm immediately covered her abdomen. Her face tensed. "'All...all right'?"

''Relax, it's just routine. She'll check you out, maybe even let you listen to the little one's heartbeat.''

''You don't think anything is wrong?''

''I'm sure it's not. You're just a little…thin, is all. She'll probably give you some vitamins or something.'' His smile was wide, bright, reassuring and totally false.

Thin? She tried to remember how many full meals— much less healthy ones—she had eaten before she took up with the ranger. Other than the mango and bananas that grew plentifully in San Ynez, fruits and vegetables were hard to come by, fresh meat almost nonexistent. Mostly she lived off dried beans and canned meat. Food that could be packed quickly and carried easily from camp to camp.

Inside the office building, Del spoke quietly to the nurse at the front desk. The woman's hair was bleached white, and she wore pink scrubs with teddy bears floating in clouds and looked at Elisa sympathetically.

Elisa stared at her feet self-consciously. She sat in a chair in the waiting area and picked up a magazine. Seconds later she had forgotten about the nurse and was engrossed in an article titled The Healthy Pregnancy. The article was illustrated, and the women's swollen bodies fascinated her. Would she really look like that soon? For all her education, she was woefully ignorant about what was happening to her own body. That ignorance made her uncertain, vulnerable, and she was too much the survivor to accept vulnerability. She devoured that article, then another, on breast-feeding, but the more she read, the more she realized she needed to learn.

She started when the ranger touched her on the shoulder.

''Sorry,'' he said, handing her a clipboard. ''But they need some information from you.''

She scanned the form, her stomach twisting.

"I explained that you, uh…might not know some of the information. That you haven't had much medical care lately."

She filled in the blanks she knew—childhood illnesses, vaccination history and hereditary conditions in her family—and left the rest blank, except for the date of conception. Her cheeks heating, she scribbled in a date and handed the clipboard to Del just as a second nurse, this one in surgical greens, pushed open a door and called her name.

Bracing herself with a breath, she straightened her back and walked toward the nurse. Del followed.

Elisa stopped, shaking her head. "No."

He glanced toward the exam room door where the nurse waited, then back to Elisa. "You sure?"

"This baby is my responsibility." She watched him hook his big hands in his belt and remembered those big hands tending his yellow roses with such loving care. "I take care of what's mine," she mimicked his words, turned them to her own meaning to keep him in the waiting room where he belonged. This was a private matter.

Dr. Marsala was Indonesian. She had a large nose, soft voice and gentle hands. The pelvic exam was completed efficiently and painlessly, and Elisa was prepped for the big moment, the sonogram where she would first see her baby.

"Are you frightened," the doctor asked as she spread warm gel on Elisa's abdomen.

"Yes."

Dr. Marsala smiled. "Good. If you had said no, I would have known you were lying."

A computer blinked next to the examination table, and

the doctor tapped a series of commands on the attached keyboard. The gray display on the monitor wavered, then stabilized. Elisa's name and the date appeared at the bottom of the picture.

"What you're going to see is live video of your child. Or at least live video of sound waves bouncing off your child's mass."

"Will you be able to tell if it's healthy?"

"We can detect some conditions at this stage, but mostly we're just looking at the fetus's size and shape to give us an idea how it's developing."

The doctor pressed a flat wand lightly into the goo covering Elisa's stomach. Compared to the warm gel, the plastic was cold. The muscles in her abdomen rippled in reaction. Undeterred, the doctor concentrated on the computer monitor, studying gray and black masses as she moved the wand over Elisa.

"There," Dr. Marsala declared, smiling and pointing at a blob on the screen. "There's the sac."

Elisa couldn't make anything of the picture, but she smiled, too. Her heart accelerated.

Slowly Dr. Marsala moved the wand down and to Elisa's left, then back. Then again. "There we are. I can't tell if it's a girl or boy in this position, but there's the head, the chest." She outlined a vaguely human shape on the screen with her free hand. "See the little legs and arms forming?"

Elisa's breath stalled as she stared at the tiny being growing inside her. This baby is her responsibility, she'd told Del, and for the first time she was beginning to understand what that meant. To understand the commitment. The joy and the grief, the love and the fierce protectiveness this child brought out in her.

"Is it okay?" she asked, choking back the emotion. "Is the baby healthy?"

The doctor moved the wand to the right a fraction. Her smile remained frozen in place, but she drew her brows together.

Elisa's fingers dug into the sides of the bed. "What is it? What's wrong with my baby?"

Chapter 5

Del had seen Elisa in noble-jungle-princess mode, cool, aloof and wearing her pride like a crown jewel. And he'd seen her as the warrior queen, full of passionate fury and righteous indignation at the injustices done her.

The Elisa who'd walked out of the women's center with him fifteen minutes ago clutching a grainy black-and-white printout from her sonogram and a pack of vitamins was neither.

This was the vulnerable Elisa. The one he'd caught a glimpse of in the cemetery chapel before she'd realized he was there, and again on her knees on the side of the road, purging her stomach over a steel guardrail.

This was the Elisa who haunted his sleep. Who shredded his gut to bloody ribbons with a single look and left his soul in tatters every time she referred to him as ''Ranger'' instead of by his given name.

This was the Elisa he couldn't let walk away. Despite her insistence she could take care of herself, sending her off alone would be like throwing a kitten into a junkyard full of rabid dogs.

The problem was he didn't have any choice. Even if she wasn't an American citizen, she still had rights. He couldn't hold her against her will. They were almost at the bank, and he couldn't think of any way to keep her from leaving him once they were done there, other than driving his Land Rover into a tree, which didn't seem like a smart plan, given her pregnancy.

He clutched the steering wheel until his fingers cramped, then flexed the digits, glancing at Elisa from behind his aviator sunglasses. She was still staring at the sonogram picture as if it was the key to the mystery of life.

In a way it was, he supposed. The first look at a new life. He couldn't tell butt-from-backside in the picture, and still a flutter of emotion rippled through his chest at the sight of it. He couldn't begin to imagine how Elisa must feel, seeing her baby for the first time. Knowing that little being was growing inside her.

Judging by her rounded shoulders and the pinched lines at the corners of her mouth, it must be overwhelming.

"You look wiped out," he said, noting how thin and colorless her lips looked. "Maybe we should put off this bank thing for a few hours. Go home and have lunch, get some rest first."

She didn't look up, just mumbled, "Yes, you are probably right."

Del damn near did run his Rover into a tree. Jerking the vehicle to a stop on the side of the road, he gave her a long look. More than just her lips had lost their color. The flesh beneath her fingernails was white, and the picture she held trembled in her unsteady hand.

"What's wrong?" he asked more gruffly than he'd intended.

When she finally looked up at him, her eyes as bleak as a picture of a nature preserve after a forest fire. "You were correct the other night. I cannot take your money. It would not be right."

"Honey, I think you're taking this motherhood thing a little too seriously. This is no time for you to develop a conscience." He laced the words with sarcasm. Meant them as a joke.

Only, Elisa wasn't laughing. To Del's horror her eyes swelled with tears.

"Aw, God damn it. Don't cry."

She flinched at his expletive, made the sign of the cross, and he cursed himself again silently. He knew she had a thing about using the Lord's name. Hell, he respected her for it.

She held her tears in check, though Del didn't know how, her eyes were so full. "I won't take your money," she said, her hands twining in her lap. "It would be wrong."

When she looked up, she seemed calmer, but still devastated. Her voice dropped to a whisper. "But if your other offer still stands…"

Del's jaw fell slack. "You want to marry me?"

"Yes." She met his eyes levelly. God, she was incredible. Her pride. Her strength.

Too bad he knew she was lying. "What the hell happened in the doctor's office?"

No way was he buying this change of heart without a reason. A cold knot of fear settled where his heart ought to be while he waited for her answer. An answer he was very much afraid he wouldn't like.

Elisa's shoulders shuddered. She bit her lip until they steadied, then answered. "She said that I am anemic."

Del blew out a breath. "Anemic. That's not so bad. Pretty normal during pregnancy. She gave you vitamins, right? And an iron supplement?"

Elisa nodded. "Except she said I am very anemic. Probably due to stress and a poor diet. She said it was so bad that it might be affecting the baby."

Her tears returned. The knot in Del's chest expanded into a beach ball, inflated past its capacity and ready to blow.

"She said my baby is too small for its gestational age." Elisa's face hardened, then cracked, and the tears spilled over onto her cheeks. "She said it might not be growing enough to survive."

"Aw, 'Lis." He took her shoulders and pulled her head to his chest, even more deeply disturbed by the fact that she let him.

She felt cold and stiff in his arms, her emotions all closed off, pent-up inside her, but he knew she couldn't stave off her emotions forever. No one could.

The first tremor broke through with an audible rattling of her teeth. Her control splintered rapid-fire from there, releasing her shudders in a series of jagged convulsions that speared Del's heart.

He held on to her so tightly he was afraid he might hurt her. "It's all right. Gonna be okay."

She quivered against him, and he planted a kiss in her hair as her shoulders shook. God, she was killing him. She tied his lungs in bow knots. He couldn't stand to see her hurt so much.

She gulped down a choking breath, burrowed her nose against his collarbone. "It is my fault the baby is in danger. I…I thought I could take care of myself."

''You can. But you don't have to. Not now.''

''I do not like being dependent on others.''

He smiled into her hair. ''Yeah, I figured that out.''

''I would—'' Her body shook again. He rubbed her back to warm her. ''Would never have come here if Eduardo had not insisted it was the best thing for the baby.''

''It still is.'' He eased back and tipped her head up to where he could see her, framing her face with both hands. ''Honey, I'm sorry about Eduardo. I would give anything to bring him back if I could. But I can't. You've got to let me help you now.''

The last of her tremors fading, she nodded reluctantly. ''The doctor said I must rest and eat well.''

''I have a big bed,'' he said, pushing away the image of her lying in it all alone. ''And plenty of food.''

She studied the dome light above his head, then brought her gaze down to his. ''If I lose the baby, there is no reason for me to stay in the United States.''

He knew what she was doing. Letting him off the hook. Giving him an excuse to take back his offer. To say, ''Let's wait and see.''

Like hell.

He clamped her head back on his shoulder. ''Don't you worry. You're going to be in Texas a long, long time.''

She'd already lost too much because of him, he thought fiercely. She wouldn't lose her child, too. Not without one hell of a fight.

Elisa stretched her arms over her head, rolled to her side and pressed her cheek deeper into the pillow. The Ranger's pillow. As if he instinctively understood that her fledgling trust did not extend yet to his friend, the politician, he had not brought her back to the big house, but to his own small apartment. His bed. She could smell him there, in the sheets. Sandalwood aftershave and cocoa butter soap. The sensation was so real she thought if she reached out—without opening her eyes—she could touch his short brown hair. She could trace the crescent furrows that bracketed his mouth when he smiled.

A rap on the door roused her from her twilight sleep musings in time to see Del shoulder his way into the room, a tray laden with food and smelling scrumptious balanced in his hands. She sat bolt upright, smoothing the ruffled covers as if afraid he would see what she had been imagining.

The guilt hit her a second later. Shame raked her cheeks. What was wrong with her, thinking of the ranger in that way? She had come to this country to be with Eduardo. It was to him she owed her loyalty still.

Even if it was the ranger's ring she would one day wear.

Squaring her shoulders and lifting her chin, she propped herself up on a pillow.

"I hope you're hungry," the ranger said as he set the tray in her lap.

The single yellow rose in a thin vase in the corner brought a lump to her throat. "This is all for me?"

"Every bite."

She lifted the paper plate turned upside down over the center dish. "Eggs?"

He removed the cover from a side plate. "And steak. A Texas breakfast tradition."

"Breakfast?" Her gaze leaped to the window, where sunlight gleamed off the spotless glass. It seemed only minutes had passed since she'd lain down for a short catnap at dusk. She read the glowing numbers on the digital clock on the nightstand to verify. It was nearly 9:00 a.m. She'd slept twelve straight hours.

"Time for your iron pill." He nodded toward a dime-size tablet and handed her the glass of juice from her tray. While she swallowed, he picked up the knife and began cutting the steak.

"I can do it," she said, trying to take the knife.

"Indulge me."

She sat back uneasily. She was not accustomed to being pampered, but as she watched him skewer and chop the meat into precise centimeter cubes, she found the experience was not altogether unpleasant.

He looked up at her and smiled. He seemed at ease with the closeness. The intimacy of preparing another's food. It made her wonder…

"Have you been married before, Ranger?"

"No. And since we're going to be married soon, do you think you could call me Del?"

"Del." It was a nice name. She just wasn't sure she could bring herself to use it. Referring to him as "Ranger" offered a comfortable measure of distance. Breathing room. "Why have you never married?"

He shrugged. "Just never found the right person, I guess."

She took her time studying him while he was occupied with her meal. He wasn't unattractive. His broad, square features suited his strength. His character. She didn't imagine him having trouble finding a woman.

"That's not it," she challenged, and flaked the top layer off her eggs with the tip of her fork. "What is this green stuff."

"Spinach. Lots of iron. Eat it."

"When you tell me why you never married."

Setting the knife on the tray with a clank, he sighed lustily. "So that's the way it's going to be? Blackmail?"

The words were ominous, but his mercurial eyes danced.

She speared a forkful of eggs and lifted it to her mouth, circling just in front of her curved lips, waiting. Her smile fell when he pulled his face into a worried frown and shrank back to the edge of the mattress.

"I was hoping to spare you this," he said, gazing out the window.

Her stomach lurched. Her hand sagged, and the bite of eggs fell back to the plate.

"But I guess you would've found out, anyway, sooner or later. Might as well get it out in the open from the start."

Elisa'a heart hammered. She was both afraid to hear what he had to say and afraid not to.

"It's a medical condition," he said fiercely, as if he dared her to deny it.

"Oye," she breathed. "What is it?"

"I'm afraid I suffer from a chronic case of domestic commitment avoidance."

Elisa gaped.

"Complicated by frequent bouts of foul-temperitis and cursing-habit disease."

A laugh broke from Elisa's chest, followed by another.

"Sometimes when it's really bad, I even take the Lord's name in vain."

"I noticed," she said, hiding her giggles behind a fake cough.

"You see? There's not a woman in Texas who'll have me."

"Except me."

He took the fork from her hand, pinned a bite of steak

on the end and raised it to her mouth. His eyes turned serious. "You, I figure, are just stubborn enough to put up with me."

She opened her mouth to argue, but he popped the meat in before she got a word out.

"Who knows, maybe you'll even cure me."

She chewed slowly, savoring the taste of tender steak and the tender look in the ranger's eyes equally. Somehow his gaze warmed her from the inside out. Shone light on dark places inside her she had forgotten existed. Gradually the heat rose to an uncomfortable level. Blood rushed to her cheeks and she was forced to look away.

When he caught her gaze again, he was smiling.

"Are you sure you want to do this?" she asked softly, shyly.

"Marry you?"

She nodded, unable to say the word. What he proposed was not really a marriage, after all, but more like a business arrangement. A two-year payment on a debt.

"As sure as there's gonna be mosquitoes in Texas after it rains," he said cockily, then sobered. He put his hand over the bulge that held her baby. She sucked in a breath as the muscles in her abdomen fluttered under his touch and she felt another tiny stirring, deeper.

"As sure as I am of this healthy, beautiful baby girl you're going to have."

"It is a boy."

"Girl."

"You do not know."

"Neither do you."

"I can feel it."

"I can see it. I told you, my grandmother is a midwife. I've seen a lot of women before and after they've had their babies. Yours is a girl."

"We will see," she said stiffly. She had never considered that she carried anything other than Eduardo's son. More so since he was killed.

Not that the sex of her baby was important. Its health was what was important. But still...a girl...

She smiled.

The ranger pulled his hand away abruptly and stood. "Now eat your breakfast so we can hit the road. The car's already packed."

Lost, she followed his back across the room with her gaze. "Where are we going?"

At the door he stopped and turned. "To get some advice from a lady who knows more about bringing babies into this world than anyone else in the state, doctors included. My grandmother."

Del was convinced that the Cooper farm, thirty-five acres nestled in a pecan grove in rural Van Zandt County, Texas, existed in a time warp. Every time he came, the potholes in the gravel drive were a little deeper, the creek was a little dryer, and his mother's hair a little grayer, but nothing really changed.

The rope he'd swung on a thousand times as a kid still hung in the hayloft. Grandma and Grandpa Cooper's rockers still sat facing each other on the narrow wraparound porch surrounding the farmhouse.

And his mother still didn't know who he was.

Or at least *when* he was.

Wisps of salt-and-pepper hair trailed from the bun curled atop her head as she waved at him from the front steps. "Del? Oh, Del, where have you been? I've been so worried."

He opened the door on Elisa's side of the car and

helped her down. His mother peered at them, then started forward.

Damn. He should have explained to Elisa about his mother. He'd had an hour and a half on the drive out here from Dallas, but somehow he'd never found the words. He'd been too busy trying to figure out how he was going to break the news of his impending marriage to his grandparents.

"Look," he said hurriedly. "I should have told you about my mom—"

"Del, is that Sammy with you?" Ariel Cooper asked, shading her eyes from the sun. "I sent Sammy out looking for you, you were gone so long."

"No, Mom. It's not Sammy."

Sammy hadn't been here for a long time.

"You know you're not supposed to wander off without telling me," his mother chided, then stopped when she reached Elisa.

"Oh, hello." She turned to Del with vacant eyes. "Del, are you going to introduce me to your little friend?"

Elisa looked at him curiously and he only hoped she could read his silent plea for understanding. His mom was easily confused, and he didn't want her upset.

"Mom, this is Elisa."

"Pleasure to meet you, Elisa," she said in a singsongy, childlike voice. "Are you in Del's class at the elementary?"

"No, I—"

"She's new in town, Mom. We don't know which class she'll be in yet."

"Well, won't it be fun if they put her in your class?" She gave her attention back to Elisa. "You're welcome to stay for supper. If it's all right with your parents, of course."

"It's, uh, all right, Mom," Del said.

"Well, good then. We're having pot roast. I'll just go set an extra plate." She started toward the house, and Del and Elisa followed. "You're sure you didn't see Sam out there anywhere, Del?"

Del kicked the dirt as fresh pain exploded along long-abused nerve endings. "No, Ma."

"Probably out chasing that old dog again," she said as she stepped onto the front porch and walked right past an aging border collie—a direct descendant of the dog in question.

Elisa gave him that raised-eyebrow look again as they followed his mother into the house.

"Later," he said, and it seemed to satisfy her.

His grandparents, Ian and Rosario Cooper were waiting in the kitchen.

"Del, m'boy," his pap called in a Scottish brogue as thick as the day he'd left the highlands. Balancing himself with one hand on the countertop, he hopped across the room on his one remaining leg. He'd lost the other to shrapnel in World War II, and he didn't like to wear the prosthetic limb the VA hospital had given him. Claimed his empty trouser leg was a badge of honor. Wanted people to know what he and men like him had given for their country. "How goes the fight?"

Del leaned into the offered bear hug, careful not to unbalance the elderly man. "Not much fighting to be done, Pap. I'm still on administrative leave."

"Ah, hogwash, that," Pap said, waving his hand in rude gesture. "What's a man supposed to do but shoot at the enemy?"

"Ignore el soldado viejo, Delgado, y venga a ver tu

abuela.'' Ignore the old soldier, and come to your grandmother.

Del eased from Pap's embrace and knelt beside Rosario Cooper's chair. She was a foot shorter than him,
her knuckles were swollen with arthritis, and her once
jet-black hair was now riddled with gray, yet he would
have no more dared to disobey her than he would have
jumped on the back of a Brahma bull for a joyride.

"Es bueno verle otra vez, abuela.'' He rarely spoke
Spanish these days, but when he did it never failed to
make her smile.

She touched his cheek with the back of her hand.
"Eres un muchacho bueno, Delgado.''

He captured her hand in his and rose, looking back at
Elisa. "Pap, Mami, this is my friend Elisa.''

"Elisa might be in Del's class when school starts up
again,'' his mother chimed in, pulling the pot roast from
the oven.

Long used to her eccentricity, Pap and Mami continued on as if there was nothing odd about the remark.
They each welcomed Elisa, made small talk while dinner
was served and eaten and stayed at the table after Del's
mother excused herself to go upstairs and work on the
new curtains she was sewing for the den.

Del picked up the plates, rinsed them in the sink and
measured two scoops of grounds into the coffeemaker.

This was the family routine. Supper was for pleasant
conversation.

Serious discussions were held over coffee.

When three cups—plus one glass of milk for Elisa—
had been poured and sipped, Del took his seat.

"Pap, Mami. Elisa and I have something to tell you.''

"Only one thing I want to know,'' Pap said, squinting
out of one eye. When he'd been a kid, Del had called

that look Pap's Popeye face, and it meant it was time to come clean with whatever latest prank he and Sammy had cooked up.

"What's that, Pap?" he asked, suspecting he already knew the answer.

Pap put his hand over Elisa's on the table. "I want to know if that's your baby your pretty young friend is carrying, and if it is, why there isn't a ring on her finger?"

Elisa choked, almost spewing milk across the table.

Mami leaned over to pat her on the back. *"Querida, take a deep breath."* She glared at Pap. "Ian, you have embarrassed *la niña.*"

"She's not the one who should be embarrassed," Pap said, impaling Del with a look. "What do you have to say, son? Are you going to honor your responsibilities and do right by this woman, or not?"

Del was trying. "Actually, Pap, that's what we wanted to tell you. Elisa and I are—"

Mami raised her hands out to her sides and tipped her head to the heavens. Her smile lit up the room. "Of course they are getting married. They're having a baby!" Tears flowing, she leaned over and kissed Elisa on both cheeks.

Elisa's panic-stricken, dark eyes locked on Del's like laser-guided missiles. He raised his eyebrows in defense.

"See how they look at each other?" Mami exclaimed, joy bursting from every word. "They are in love."

Del cursed himself for losing control of the conversation. He should have known Mami and Pap would assume Elisa's baby was his. What else would they think? He'd never brought a woman—any woman, much less one in her second trimester of pregnancy—home before.

Clearly, Elisa wanted him to straighten them out.

"Think of it, Ian," Mami said, her hands clasped to her chest. "A grandchild. Our first grandchild."

"Actually, the baby isn't…" Del began, but hesitated. This was where he should do it. Tell his grandparents the baby wasn't his. The marriage would be legal, but it wouldn't be real. That Elisa only stayed with him because she feared for her baby's life. That underneath the pleasant mask she'd donned for their benefit, she loathed the sight of him, and with good reason.

But looking at his grandparents now, he couldn't do it. Satisfaction beamed from his grandfather's face. Mami's eyes shone with such unconditional love and acceptance that it made his chest ache. As a kid he used to wonder what he'd done to deserve that kind of love. To deserve them.

As an adult, he still didn't know.

He did know they had faced a lot of sadness in their lives. He couldn't shatter this moment of happiness, even if its source was only an illusion.

He met Elisa's level gaze. Her nostrils flared. A warning? He sent a look he hoped she would recognize as a silent apology, and a plea…

"Actually, the baby isn't your grandchild," he finished the statement he'd started earlier, only not the way he'd originally planned. "It would be your great-grandchild."

Elisa rose. Del held his breath, waiting for her to cut the hearts out of two of the finest people on Earth, but she merely turned her back on the table and took her empty glass to the sink.

"Ach, so it will. You were so young when you came to live with us that you've always been like a son."

Papi's brogue was thicker than usual, choked with emotion. "And now we have a daughter, too."

Judging by the way Elisa's spine stiffened at Pap's declaration, Del wasn't so sure she agreed.

Chapter 6

"One hopscotch, two hopscotch, three hopscotch," Del's mother sang as she skipped her red checker across the board, stacking Elisa's last black pieces beneath it as she went. "I win again."

Elisa pulled her gaze from the baseball game playing out on the TV in the corner with the sound turned down, and frowned at the checkerboard.

"Don't take it too hard, sweetie. You did good for a beginner. Del and Sammy have been trying to beat me since they learned to play in Bible camp three years ago, and they haven't come as close as you did." She looked toward the window. "Now where have those boys gotten to?"

"I'm here, Ma."

The ranger's voice, soft and heavy, fell on Elisa like a shower of tiny, electrified raindrops. It wasn't like her to be so affected by something as mundane as a man's voice, even if he had surprised her. Perhaps it was not the voice, but the sadness she heard in it. The humanity.

As she turned toward him, she rubbed the gooseflesh from her bare arms. She didn't want to think of the ranger as human. Especially not after he had broken their agreement.

"Did Sammy come in with you?" his mother asked.

The shadow of his eyelashes fluttered on his cheek as he half closed his eyes. "No, Ma."

"I'll just go call him, then." The ranger moved aside as his mother walked out. She laughed on her way past him, but it was an anxious sound. Her fingers twisted in the skirt of her cotton dress. "Boy's prob'ly out chasin' that old dog again."

When Mrs. Cooper was gone, Elisa bent over the checkerboard and started picking up the pieces. She heard the shoosh of the ranger's boots over the carpet. Felt the air compress around her as he drew up beside her. Watched her numb fingers give over the checkers without resistance when he gathered her hands in his.

In the place of the plastic game pieces, he put a steaming mug.

"From my grandmother. She says to drink as much of this as you can stand tonight, and tomorrow she'll have a whole nutritional plan worked out for you."

"You lied to them," she said.

"Not exactly." He sat on the floor, his long legs stretched out to one side and propped on his elbow, and motioned her toward the love seat. One by one, he set each checker in its place.

Incredulity spilled over her. "Then you misled them."

He moved his first checker and gestured for her turn. "That's what this marriage is about, isn't it? Misleading people?"

"But these are your family."

He sighed. "I tried to tell them the truth. I just…couldn't. You saw how excited my grandmother was."

Elisa contemplated the game a moment, then nudged a checker forward. "And when she does find out?"

"I've got two years to figure that out."

"Maybe." Del took his turn, and Elisa interpreted his strategy. He'd opened with a direct frontal assault. She would have expected no less. Countering with a flanking move, she said, "Your grandmother is very astute. Do you think she will not notice something is wrong before then?"

Del frowned in concentration, whether on the game or the discussion, Elisa could not tell. "We'll just have to make it look real."

Her stomach tumbled, imaging what it would be like even to *pretend* to be in love with him. She would have to talk to him, share long looks with him, touch him…

"It won't be that bad," he said, as if sensing the direction of her thoughts. "We don't have to be together around them that much. Just holidays and such."

"I would like to spend more time here," she said before she realized she was speaking. In just a few short hours, she had come to respect the ranger's grandparents. Rosario Cooper reminded her of home, and the elder women she had learned so much from in her village as a girl.

The ranger grinned over his next move. "They like you, too."

"They do?" She hadn't realized until then how much their acceptance meant to her. She still didn't understand why. Like the ranger, they would be her family in name only. And only for two years.

With the weight of that knowledge rumbling through her like thunder down a mountain pass, she studied the checkerboard. The ranger had taken two of her men in a sneak attack. He was good. But she was better.

She proved it by winning their best three-of-five match in three straight games.

"I think I've been conned," he said, falling backward and staring up at the ceiling.

His good-natured tone made her smile, just a little, even though she was still mad at him.

She folded the checkerboard and gathered the pieces. He sat up, opened the coffee table drawer where they were stored. When she slid the game inside, he nudged the drawer closed with his knee, took hold of her with his hand and turned her to him.

"Thank you," he said simply.

She arched one eyebrow. "For beating you?"

"For not telling my grandparents the truth." One corner of his mouth kicked up. "And for letting my mother win at checkers."

Elisa pulled her hand away. "I am not without compassion."

"No," he answered quietly. "You're certainly not."

She wondered how he knew that. She certainly hadn't shown him much of her softer side. Hadn't seen much of it herself these last eight years.

Avoiding his gaze, she straightened the magazines on the coffee table, then when she couldn't find anything else to fidget with, she settled herself on the love seat again. Something in the way he was looking at her evaporated her troubled thoughts like morning mist under the rising sun. But she gathered her wits, kicking off her sandals and pulling her feet up to the couch.

He'd opened a door, given her space to ask a personal

question, and she did not intend to let the opportunity pass.

"What happened to her?"

"My mother?"

She nodded.

"She lost a lot of people she loved during her life, starting with her parents when she was just sixteen. I guess one day she just lost herself, as well."

Dread knotted in Elisa's chest. "Sammy?"

A darkness descended over the ranger's features, like a candle suddenly snuffed. "My brother. Killed by a suicide bomber in Saudi Arabia during the Gulf War."

"He was a soldier?"

"We both were."

Elisa tried to swallow and couldn't. In San Ynez, the soldiers were even worse than the police. More corrupt. More violent.

The ranger's grandfather had been a soldier, as had he and his brother. A legacy of violence.

And there was more, Elisa suspected from the degree of his mother's devastation, though the loss of a child should be enough. "Your father?"

"Pilot. Drove an A-10—a tank killer—in Vietnam until he was shot down in '68. Technically he's still listed as MIA."

"And the not knowing was harder on her than having a body to bury."

Elisa was all too familiar with the plight of families left without closure. She'd seen too many of them in her country.

The ranger studied the carpet between his feet. Quiet surrounded the house—even the crickets had hushed for the night. "She thinks she still gets letters from him."

The grate in his voice reminded her that he had lost much, too. A father, a brother, and a mother in a way.

"Sometimes when she gets upset at not hearing from him, I go and get one of his old letters out of the box she keeps upstairs and I read it to her."

Elisa's heart throbbed. Mesmerized by the story, by the depth of the emotion that resonated in its telling, she leaned forward.

He pinched his lips bloodless before he spoke again. "She never seems to notice that the envelope is already torn open or that she's heard the words a hundred times before."

Elisa reached out, but stopped short of touching him. Instead she rested her hand just beyond his splayed fingers. "You are a good son."

"Am I?" Heat and light flashed from him like a small explosion. He leaned toward her, his palms supporting his weight on the table. "For letting her live in her goddamn fantasy world instead of shaking her back to reality?"

Elisa reared back, not just from his fury, but to make the sign of the cross and wing a quick prayer of forgiveness heavenward.

He rolled his head back and scrubbed his hands over his face, muffling something she suspected would require more than a quick prayer to be forgiven.

"You're a real stickler on the swearing thing, aren't you?"

"It is the way I was raised."

A breath sagged out of him. "It's the way I was raised, too. Guess I'd just forgotten."

He stood and offered her a hand. "I'll try to remember from now on."

Once he had lifted her to her feet, he lingered with

her hand in his. She wondered if he could feel the way her pulse spiraled at his touch.

"If you're up to it tomorrow," he said, "we'll go into town, apply for a marriage license, get blood tests."

Her pulse went from spiraling to bounding. Her stomach sank in on itself, but she held her ground.

The ranger's gaze met hers, solid as rock. "We'll be married before the week is out."

Elisa woke as she had each morning at the Cooper farm, enamored with the crinkle of fresh linens under her cheek, the smell of freshly brewed coffee tickling her nose—not that she could have any—and the warmth of golden sunlight flowing through gauzy curtains.

Not to mention the sight of a large, half-naked male laboring outside her window, which was about as close as he'd gotten to her since their discussion over checkers in the den four nights ago.

The ranger tended his grandmother's vegetable garden before the heat of the day set in. Wearing only jeans, boots and a leather belt with a silver buckle the size of a soup ladle, he knitted the limbs of a leggy tomato plant into a wire cage, mounded a burm of soil around the base of a flowering pepper plant and checked an ear of yellow corn for insects.

Even at this hour, exertion and the Texas heat had him sweating. His bare torso shone like a new bronze statue. Muscles bunched like mountains of pure stone in his shoulders and taut flesh played over an abdomen hammered flat as a platter. When he squatted to finger the frothy topside of a carrot plant, his thighs tested the seams of the denim that encased them.

He looked at home there among the rows and patches, she realized, and that was the appeal of watching him.

He looked like a man who lived by his hands instead of his gun. A peaceable man, capable of coaxing life from a handful of seeds and a square of dry soil, of nurturing tender green shoots into sturdy stalks. A man with the patience, and the strength, to wait for the time to reap the bounty of what he had sown.

Not at all like the reckless policeman who took an innocent life by mistake. The impulsive repentant who, out of guilt, offered marriage to a stranger. Committed himself to raise another man's child.

This was a new ranger. One who read his dead father's old letters again and again as if they were new to comfort a mother who lived in the past. One who mourned a lost brother. Father.

One who promised her that her baby would be all right with such sincerity that she almost believed he could make it so.

Restlessly Elisa pushed the covers aside and swung her legs over the side of the bed. She took her iron tablet with a cup of Mami's miracle tea in the kitchen, but passed up the spinach and tomato omelet the elder Mrs. Cooper pressed on her.

Each of the last three days, she'd eaten with the elder Coopers and Del's mother while he worked in the garden or tended livestock. In the afternoon she watched baseball with Mami. Mami was a die-hard fan, and Elisa was surprised to learn she enjoyed the game, as well.

Each evening she'd taken supper with them while Del again found chores to do. And after sunset, she'd displaced the family dog, Murphy, who she was told was named after a famous soldier, Audie Murphy, from the easy chair in the family room and curled up with a book borrowed from the floor-to-ceiling shelves. She had half hoped the ranger would join her there, as he had the night they had played checkers, and tried to deny her disappointment when he had not. That night, he had opened up to her, shared something of himself.

The single draught of information left her thirsting for more.

Her nerves quivered as she padded out of the house toward the lot of tilled earth where he worked.

She was tired of waiting for him to come to her. She needed to know more about the man she was to marry, and there were things he needed to know about her.

Before four o'clock this afternoon, when the ceremony was to begin.

Hunched over in a row of green peas, Del watched Elisa's long, tanned legs swing toward him one enticing step at a time. Her calves were firm, tapering into fine ankles. Slender, with lots of definition to the bone.

He'd always been an ankle man.

"Don't touch that crabgrass," he ordered, pulling his gaze away from her ankles when she bent over next to him. Without looking up, he nudged her away with his knuckles. Her skin looked soft and white and thin as paper next to his dirty hand, but he recognized the illusion. Underneath she was strong as a jungle cat.

His paper lioness.

"I want to help."

He pinched the offending weed by the root and yanked. "You're supposed to be taking it easy."

"If I took it any easier, I would be comatose."

He craned his head back, squinting against the sun's glare. "Did you just make a joke?"

She pulled her shoulders up defensively and cocked her jaw to the side. "I do have a sense of humor."

He didn't. Not with Elisa standing over him, her

glossy black hair combed back and secured with a braided headband, her golden skin glowing and her cheeks blooming like pink roses. Especially not with the way the sun behind her shone through the white cotton shift she wore, outlining the plump of her breasts, a waist narrow despite her pregnancy and hips with just enough flare to tempt a saint.

And Del Cooper was no saint.

He wasn't much of a comedy fan, either. But he doubted Elisa would have come looking for him without reason. She had something on her mind.

He stood, brushed the dirt from his knees. "Come on, then. Let's go someplace cool and you can try to make me laugh."

Murphy trailed them to the barn. Del stretched out on some old bales of straw. Elisa settled on the wooden grain bin in her typical perfect posture, her fine ankles and knees together, back straight and hands folded in her lap. Dust motes sailed aimlessly by and a dozen starlings swooped and chattered in the rafters while Del waited for her to speak her mind.

"What I have to say is not funny," she finally admitted.

"I didn't think it would be." He plucked a piece of straw and popped the end in his mouth.

"Perhaps we should not get married this afternoon."

"Why not?"

She studied one thumbnail intensely. "We still do not know about the baby. If it will…be all right. If there is no baby, there is need to be married."

He stopped chewing the ragged end of his straw and sat up. "Have you looked in a mirror lately?"

She raised her gaze to his. He felt the churn in her coffee eyes deep in the pit of his stomach.

"Why?" she asked tentatively, as if afraid to hear the answer. Afraid something else was wrong, and she hadn't noticed.

"You look like the picture of perfect health." And of the perfect woman. "The dark circles are gone from your eyes, and the color is back in your face. It looks to me like you've put on a few pounds—all right where that baby is growing. You are both going to be fine."

She shook her heard slowly. "You cannot be sure."

"I am." The intensity in his voice—and the certainty in his heart—surprised him. He refused to acknowledge any other possibility. "Bank on it."

Her chest rose and fell in a deep but silent breath. "You do not have to do this."

"Are you trying to convince me of that, or yourself?"

"You did not mean to harm Eduardo. It was an accident. You owe me nothing."

"I owe you everything." The self-recrimination that had lain quiet inside him these last few days, soothed by the peace of the farm, seethed in the pit of his stomach like a nest of water moccasins. "Look, I know you loved Garcia, and I'm no replacement for him, but—"

"I did not."

He stopped, his mouth open, waiting for his brain to catch up. Surely he'd mistaken her meaning.

"I did not love Eduardo."

There wasn't much to mistake about that.

"I did not know him well enough to love him," she explained, her voice dropping to a whisper.

"But you knew him well enough to have his baby."

She jolted lightly at his words, and with good cause. The accusation in them had been clear, if unintentional.

"It is Garcia's baby, isn't it?"

Her head snapped up. Her eyes blazed black fire. ''I am many things. But I am not a whore.''

Del was many things, as well. One of them was a foul-tempered jerk.

He stood, shoved his fingers into the waistband of his jeans and paced. On the other side of the aisle, he scratched Lulu the milk cow's forelock as she chewed her cud. The animal looked at him through placid, trusting brown eyes. The world was the same to Lulu now as it had been thirty seconds ago. Nothing had changed.

Nothing had changed for Del, either, he gradually realized.

It didn't matter whether she'd loved Garcia or not. She'd planned to marry him, to raise her baby here. Del had spoiled those plans. He had to make up for it.

Love, or the lack of it, was not important.

Slowly, the pounding of his heart subsided to a few off-kilter knocks. He sat next to Elisa on the tack box. Her body tensed, as if to ward off a blow—or a man with no right to judge, passing judgment on her.

''How the hell did you get into this mess?''

Murphy got up from his spot in the sun, padded over to Elisa and put his chin in her lap. She stroked the dog's head.

''Eduardo came to San Ynez with the World Aid Organization. The villages in the San Torna mountains are poor, and they had been ravaged by floods in the spring. Many people lost their homes, their farms, their livestock, everything they had. Eduardo brought food and medical supplies.''

''Is that where you're from? The San Torna mountains?''

She shifted her eyes from the dog to the bird nest over the doorway to the cow stall, where Lulu was banging the feeder for more hay. Del wondered what made her nervous about a simple question like where she was from.

"I was there when the WAO dropped in supplies by helicopter. The villagers were frightened at first, but Eduardo earned their trust."

"And yours?" Del swallowed, turning away to hide his sour expression. Despite the fact that theirs would be a marriage of convenience, the thought of Elisa with another man left a sour taste on his tongue.

"No." She stared over his shoulder intently, as if seeing lush green mountains instead of gray plank walls. "Not then." Then she pulled her gaze down to Del's. "Not until the soldiers came."

"What did they want?" Based on Elisa's expression, he didn't think they'd come to feed the refugees.

"They were recruiting workers for the cocaine growers in the valley." Her forehead furrowed. "Anyone over the age of ten would do, and they weren't particular whether you wanted to go or not. They took old women, children. If not for *la resistáncia,* they might have taken the whole village."

A black memory crept up on Del. He couldn't see it— wouldn't let himself see it—but he felt it in the way the hairs on the back of his neck prickled. "The resistance. You mean the rebel army?"

Elisa looked a prickly herself. "They are not rebels. They are freedom fighters—when they must fight. In San Torna they freed the prisoners without violence and hid them in the hills. It is the soldiers who would rather shed blood than live in peace. In retribution the army attacked one of the villages, the one where I was, and Eduardo. They fired mortars into the streets, burned the building

where schoolchildren had done their lessons only hours
before.''

Her hands clenched on her thighs. The newly regained
color in her cheeks faded.

''Eduardo and I were trapped in the medical clinic,''
she continued. ''The *soldados* were coming. I ran across
the street, toward the forest. The muzzle of a big gun
mounted on a truck flashed. There was a roar. Then
screaming. Crying. I fell. I remember the feel of mud
beneath my cheek and blood on my hands.''

Those hands were shaking now, and Del figured his
probably were, too. His memories ran parallel to hers.
He felt the heat of the blast. Heard the shouts, the wails.
Smelled the blood.

Only he wasn't in a mountain village in San Ynez. He
was at a street café table in Saudi Arabia, drinking what
passed for coffee over there with Sam.

God, Sam…

The ache in his chest exploded like a Roman candle
on the Fourth of July. Sparks sizzled toward his extremities. His breath whistled.

Armies didn't make war on their own people, for
Christ's sake. He'd spent most of his four years in the
U.S. military stationed in Europe, Africa and the Middle
East. Invariably it was the political malcontents, the so-
called resistance, freedom fighters, people's movements
or revolutionaries who mired their countries in cycles of
violence rather than working with their governments toward peace. Rebels, no matter what name or cause they
went by, thrived on unrest. On destruction and death.

They didn't care whose.

Del resisted the urge to wipe his sweaty palms on his
jeans as if still trying to rid himself of the blood—his
brother's blood—fourteen years later. With an effort that

started a headache throbbing at the base of his skull, he turned his attention back to Elisa.

Her eyes were dry and clear, but her lips trembled as she finished her story. "The next thing I knew, I was in Eduardo's arms. He carried me across the street and lay on top of me while the soldiers shelled the clinic into rubble. Then he took me farther into the woods to join the others."

"He saved your life." As Sam had saved Del's.

She nodded. "I didn't know until the next day that he had a piece of shrapnel lodged in his back. He developed a fever. The infection almost killed him."

It wasn't hard to see where this was leading. "And you nursed him back to health."

"We stayed eleven days in the resistance encampment, until he was well enough to travel. Then we said goodbye."

"Until you found out you were pregnant."

She nodded again. "I wrote to him in the United States." Her eyes shimmered desperately. "I asked him only to take the baby, to raise the child where it would be safe. But he would not take our baby without its mother. He said he would keep us both safe. It was his duty."

"I wish…" Del struggled for words to describe the hollow place her story left inside him. Knowing what kind of man Eduardo had been only made Del feel his loss more keenly. There were far too few honorable men left in the world. Because of his mistake, there was now one less. "I wish I had known Eduardo. I think I would have liked him."

"Because you are much like him," she said softly, and she covered his hand with hers. "But it was a mistake, coming here to marry Eduardo when I hardly knew him. Perhaps all that has happened is fate's way of righting that wrong.''

''Nothing that's happened is your fault,'' he snapped.

''Marrying you would be an even bigger mistake.''

''Bigger than being deported back to San Ynez?''

''Our marriage would be a lie.'' A sad smile toyed with the corners of her mouth. ''And I am not a liar.''

''It doesn't have to be a lie.'' He reversed her grip on his hand so that it was he who held her. His heart bounced like a Mexican jumping bean, and he felt the pulse in her wrist leap in answer.

She'd said she thought she could learn to love Eduardo. His first thought had been that she could learn to love him, too, then. But that was crazy. He had killed her fiancé. Virtually kidnapped her, wrenched a promise of marriage from her and forced her into seclusion on his family farm.

When the two years were up, and her permanent residency was guaranteed, he'd be lucky if she didn't murder him in his sleep.

He decided on a safer approach than love.

''What's a marriage but a partnership? Two people who make a commitment to a common goal?'' He dared to move his hand to her belly, felt her muscles ripple under his touch and an answering contraction in his chest. Awe settled over him, and a little bit of fear. There was a life in there. A child that would be his responsibility, legally and morally, if not biologically.

In his wildest daydreams, Del had never imagined this moment. Sitting with a woman, his hand over a baby, asking—hell, practically begging—her to marry him. To change all his plans for life. Flip his priorities upside down.

He liked women well enough. Recreationally. But

he'd never planned on getting permanent with one. Never considered having a family.

Del was a soldier, as surely as he'd been when he'd worn the insignia of the Third Cavalry, United States Army. Only, now he fought the war raging on the streets of America. His life, his heart, belonged to service of his country.

And every time he looked into his mother's empty eyes he saw what it meant for a man to divide his loyalties between country and family. He never wanted to hurt a woman that way. Never wanted to leave her with nothing but a box of old letters to hold on to.

Yet here he was, feeling like one of the sheep that Murphy loved to herd. Inexorably pushed toward a destination he couldn't foresee, regret constantly circling, and guilt nipping at his heels.

The more he learned about Elisa, the more he respected her, and Eduardo. The more she tried to release him from his responsibility, the more he felt honor-bound to uphold it.

Working up what he hoped was a reassuring smile, he moved his hand away from her belly. "We have a common goal. We both want to see this baby grow up happy and safe without having to worry about mortars killing innocent people in the streets. Where is the lie in that?"

Even as he asked the question and watched her pride rise in her eyes and her concern for her child conquer it, the answer taunted him from the back of his mind.

The lie was in the wanting.

After he'd killed Eduardo, Del had told himself he only wanted to see her again so he could pay his respects to her.

Then he'd told himself he wanted to be her friend.

Today, he told them both he wanted to be her partner.

The truth was, since the moment he'd seen her, he'd just *wanted*.

Wanted her.

Chapter 7

"By the power vested in me by the state of Texas, I now pronounce you husband and wife." Justice of the Peace Clayton Billings, a rotund man with a handlebar mustache and ruddy cheeks closed the book he'd held during the ceremony.

Elisa wasn't sure if it was a Bible or an instruction manual. The J.P. had admitted this was only his second wedding in eighteen years in office.

Elisa was just happy it was over. Calm surrounded her like soap bubbles. It was done.

She had married the ranger.

At least there would be no more worrying about whether or not she should go through with it. For better or worse, she had made her decision, sealed her fate— or two years' worth, anyway.

She glanced at her new husband, wondering if he was as unsettled by the prospect as she was, but as usual he stood steady as a mountain.

The J.P. cleared his throat and grinned at Del, rocking toe to heel with the book clasped to his chest. "You may, ah, kiss the bride now."

Elisa's bubble burst. Even the ranger looked startled when he turned to her, his gray eyes roaming desperately from his grandmother, who stood with moist cheeks and a lace hanky clasped in both hands, to Elisa. She could have sworn his *abuela* was holding her breath, love shining in her eyes as she waited for her grandson's big moment.

Or what should have been the big moment.

Awkwardly Del leaned over Elisa. His breath brushed her cheek for an instant before his lips swept across hers. It was a fly-by kiss, slightly off center and totally devoid of feeling, a blunt reminder that theirs was a partnership, not a marriage.

Disappointment sank like a kite without wind in her chest. As a child, how many times had she dreamed of her wedding day? She had long ago given up the notion of white gloves, a frothy dress with a train that reached back to the third row in an historic cathedral, her new husband lifting a pearl-studded veil that made the whole ceremony look as if it was taking place in a cloud.

Life in San Ynez did not accommodate that kind of luxury.

But she had never given up the notion of love. Love did not need the trappings of a formal wedding.

It only needed passion.

Partnerships, apparently, did not. Not if that kiss was any indication.

She might have let the moment pass, keeping the loss of her childhood dreams to herself, if she hadn't seen the same feelings on his grandmother's face.

This woman had raised the Ranger as her son. She had poured her love, her life, into him. She had accepted Elisa and offered her that same love, fussing over her diet and answering endless questions about the changes her body was going through.

Mami had used her years of midwife experience to supplement the doctor's vitamin prescriptions with herbal concoctions that put weight on Elisa's bones and a glow on her face.

She had saved Elisa's baby.

Elisa loved her. She couldn't stand seeing the woman's confusion over her grandson's perfunctory display of affection.

Without daring to contemplate the consequences, she reached up, wrapped her palm around the back of his neck and pulled him down for a real kiss.

The skin at his nape was surprisingly soft for such a hard man. So was the hair that tickled her knuckles and the startled breath that puffed across her cheek in the instant before their mouths met.

None of it compared to the softness of his lips.

Tentative at first, reluctant, he played the passive role while she found the angle that fit them best. He stood unyielding while she moved her mouth against his.

Getting no response, she coaxed with a nibble. Teased with a glide of her tongue over moist, velvety male flesh. His lips were sweet and ripe as the fruit from the finest vineyard.

A door unlocked inside Elisa, the entrance to a place she had closed off long ago. The place that was feminine and sensual. That ached from too many years spent alone or with men who were her compatriots, her brothers in arms, even her friends.

But not her lovers.

With the door open, the yearning she'd locked inside rushed out. Into her veins. Through her lips. Into his.

Suddenly she wasn't kissing the ranger to please his grandmother. This was all for herself. For the woman inside her that the war in her country so rarely allowed her to set free.

Elisa raised to her tiptoes, pressing her body against the ranger, seeking the hard muscles of his chest, his hips, his thighs to balance the softness of his lips, the flutter of his eyelashes on her brow as she turned her head, smoothed her cheek against his. Her fingers banded around the iron core of his biceps as she raised up to meet him again. She mewled, probing the dark crevasse between his lips with the tip of her tongue, suckling his upper lip, then the lower one, reveling in the tremor that passed through him.

Sensing victory was close, she took his lower lip between her teeth and bore down gently.

A groan rumbled up from deep inside him. He tore his mouth away from hers. For a moment she thought he might push her away, but instead he wrapped his arms around her and jerked her closer, squeezing out every stray molecule of air between them.

His gray eyes speared her with heat, and then he took over the kiss, his lips no longer soft, but crushing. His teeth clashed with hers. His jaw worked. His tongue ravaged. Even if she had wanted to retreat, she could not have. He gave her not so much as a breath. A thought. A will of her own.

There was only need, and the sense that finally, *finally,* she didn't have to be the strong one any longer.

And then it was over.

The justice of the peace punched a button on a portable tape player, and scratchy organ music swept away the haze fogging Elisa's mind. The ranger eased her back from him, and Elisa realized he was the only thing keeping her on her feet. Her knees felt like warmed wax.

She looked up at the man who was now her husband. He had already donned an unaffected expression, but she was close enough to know better. Heat emanated from him like steam from a kettle. She felt his pulse throbbing in the grip he had on her arm.

He wasn't unaffected, she thought as he marched her out of the J.P.'s office. Not nearly.

The question was, what was he going to do about it?

Del Cooper was getting the hell out of Dodge.

He stuffed a pair of socks and a white T-shirt into his army duffel.

What had gotten into him back at the J.P.'s office? What had gotten into *her?*

Christ, who was he kidding? It wasn't her fault.

She had probably just been trying to put on a good show, in case the INS questioned the justice of the peace later.

Del was the one who had turned a simple kiss into hand-to-hand combat. Without the hands.

Just remembering the wild-berry taste of her lips, the way her breasts felt, crushed to his chest, the way her hips fit perfectly in the cradle of his was enough to make his body tighten.

He'd had no right to react the way he had. No excuse for letting his hormones run amok. Elisa Reyes—Elisa Cooper now—might be his wife. But she would never, *ever,* be his woman.

And if he really, really concentrated, maybe he could pretend he didn't regret it.

Muttering to himself about just rewards, Del cinched the drawstring on his duffel, heaved his belongings over his shoulder and turned to leave.

His mother stood in the doorway wearing a vacuous smile and looking right through him. "Did you bring your bicycle in, Del? It looks like rain."

The heat of the bright, cloudless afternoon shining through the window warmed his back. "Sure, Ma." He dropped his duffel and sat on the corner of the twin bed. "I was just coming to look for you, though."

"For me?" A spark of life lit her eyes, but quickly flickered out.

He patted the mattress next to him. She sat.

"I have to go, Ma."

He covered her hand with his where she picked at the quilted bedspread. Her bones were fine as a bird's and her pulse felt thin and watery. "I have to go back to work. Back to Dallas."

"You and Sammy." Her laugh tittered, clinked like shards of broken glass. "Always dreaming of going off places. Seeing the world."

Del propped his elbows on his knees. His head sagged between his shoulders. He wondered if she worried about him when he left like this. If she looked out into the dark, afraid her little boy was lost, or if she simply…forgot him. Out of sight, out of mind.

He hoped it was the latter.

Except, this time, forgetting wouldn't be as easy. He wasn't just leaving; he was leaving something—someone—behind as a reminder.

He scrubbed his face with his hands. His skin felt

worn, the angles of his cheeks harsher, the furrows beside his eyes deeper. "Elisa is going to stay here with you. I need you and Mami to take care of her."

His mother spun toward him, her relief evident now that the topic of conversation fit neatly into her fantasy world. "Yes, poor dear." She clasped her hands and sat next to him, leaning close and nearly whispering. "She told me she's all alone here. Of course we'll take care of her."

"Good." He wondered how his mother would integrate Elisa's baby into her alternate reality when it was born.

Undoubtedly she'd manage.

He stood, stretched down for his duffel, then remembered the envelope in his pocket. Easing himself back onto the bed, he worked up a smile. "I almost forgot. This came for you."

He didn't say when.

She drew in a sharp breath. "A letter? From your father?"

He nodded. Wanting to see her smile before he left, he'd taken it from the box upstairs before he'd started packing.

"Read it to me. Please." She tugged on his sleeve.

Del hesitated only a second, then sat down next to her. He'd read the letter so many times he could recite the words from memory, but he unfolded the note, anyway. His mom beamed at him with such love and anticipation that he wrapped an arm around her shoulders and snuggled her up close as he unfolded the letter and let the familiar shaky handwriting on the page flood him with memories.

It was the only thing he really remembered about his dad:—jagged handwriting on rumpled, stained stationery.

"May 10, 1967
Dear Ari,
Thanks for the oatmeal cookies you sent. They were mostly crumbs after the way they'd been bounced around half the globe, but they were the finest crumbs I've ever tasted. Made me think of all of us eating crackers in bed on a Saturday morning. Sure did make me homesick for you and Sam and Del…"

She had been deserted on her wedding night.

Elisa pushed a cold helping of scrambled eggs, peppered with finely diced spinach leaves and other herbs she couldn't identify, around the blue-and-white china plate in front of her.

Not that she had expected an evening of intimacy. There would never be that between her and the ranger. But she had hoped they might share a meal in private. Talk.

She hadn't expected to be abandoned on his grandmother's doorstep with hardly more than wave goodbye and a muttered promise to call.

Humiliation dragged her shoulders down. He had not even been able to meet her eyes before he left.

She had shamed herself, and him, with that kiss. He wanted nothing to do with her other than to bind his hemorrhaged honor, soothe his wounded conscience. Her brief wanton wishfulness for more appalled him.

Repulsed him.

And no wonder.

It appalled her, too.

In San Ynez, she had been the caretaker of her family and others. The villagers looked to her for direction.

Here she was as lost as a newborn lamb without its ewe.

In San Ynez, people needed her; here she was the needy one.

She did not like to admit it, but she needed the ranger—as more than a substitute husband. She needed his strength when the morning sickness swamped her. His optimism when fear for her baby's safety alarmed her.

She needed his certainty that honor still existed in the world, even if she suspected he was the last man alive who believed in it.

If he was the last honorable man, she needed him all the more for it.

Living in America, having a baby, marrying a ranger—she had no experience in these things. She did not know what to do.

Shame lumped in her throat. The blue-and-white plate before her blurred. Through the curtain of her hair, Elisa tracked the ranger's grandmother as the elderly woman crossed the kitchen. Knuckles grown bulbous with age lit on Elisa's shoulders.

"Pobrecito. ¿Qué te molesta?" What is bothering you?

Elisa raised her head and wrenched a smile onto her face for Mami's sake. "Nada, Mami. Todo está bien." Everything is fine.

Mami eased herself into the chair next to Elisa. "Never lie to an old liar, little one. Or to a woman who's put up with more than her share of trouble with men. You are here and your new husband is in Dallas. Everything cannot be fine.'' Mami patted Elisa's hand. ''So tell me what my mule-headed grandson has done.''

Elisa felt the ranger's strength in the clasp of the old woman's hand and so began, haltingly at first, to tell her story. At first she hardly dared look at Rosario Cooper, afraid of what the woman would think of her for trapping her grandson in a loveless marriage, but as the minutes passed and the understanding in Mami's eyes grew, deepened like the cool shade of the forest, the words came easier. When Elisa was done, relief lifted her like a leaf in a summer breeze.

''Can you live with him two years?'' Mami asked.

''I have lived eight years with much worse in San Ynez.''

''But you're afraid of him.''

Caution warred with the comfort that came from confiding in another woman. She hadn't told Del's grandmother everything about her life before she came to the United States. ''He is *policía*. I—''

''Not of what he represents as a Ranger. You're afraid of what he represents as a *man*.''

A quick smile, too quick, razed her mouth. ''No.''

Seven decades of wisdom were etched in the canyons carving Mami's round face. ''You are a strong one, *híja*. You had to be to survive on your own in such a harsh land. After all you've been through, it can't be easy to open your life to another. To put your future and your baby's in a stranger's hands.''

''My future and that of my baby is in my own hands.'' Her fingers closed to a fist around her fork. ''The marriage is only a formality.''

Mami fell against the back of her chair. Sunlight burnished her cheeks golden brown, like rolls fresh from the oven. "Daughter, there is nothing formal about marriage. Living with a man—the same man—day after day is like standing naked in front of a mirror. At best, you are comfortable with what you see. It's always intensely personal. There are no secrets between a woman and her mirror."

Elisa bit her lip to keep from laughing. "And at its worst?"

Mami thought a moment, then nodded to herself. "At its worst, it's like standing naked in front of one of those funhouse mirrors that make you look two feet tall and four feet wide."

A chuckle started low in Elisa's belly, near the womb where her baby slept, and climbed up. She had seen such a mirror as a child when a traveling circus had passed through the mountains. "Remind me never to go to another funhouse."

Both women laughed until their eyes watered, then gradually fell silent. Mami's hand still clasped Elisa's on the tabletop. "Whatever their reasons for entering it, a marriage is what two people make of it," she said.

Elisa steadied her quivering chin by frowning. She wasn't sure there was enough substance in her marriage to make anything. "And if only one person wants to make something?"

"My grandson is stubborn and prideful and sometimes he gets so caught up in duty that he forgets he has a responsibility to himself, his own happiness, as well. But he has a good heart. He would not have married you if he didn't think he could make some kind of life with you."

"Then why did he leave?"

"To give you a choice."

Elisa set her fork on the edge of her plate. "A choice?"

What kind of choice? Despite being twenty-eight years old, she was relatively inexperienced with men. Totally inexperienced with husbands. She had been too busy living a nightmare the past eight years to develop more than superficial relationships. Even with Eduardo.

"Maybe it's his way of finding out whether or not you want to make some kind of life with him," Mami coached gently.

Elisa looked up, frustration eking out of her. "A test? This is some sort of stupid male test of my commitment?"

"Why don't you ask him?"

"How am I supposed to do that, with him in Dallas?"

Mami arched one eyebrow in a look Elisa could only call a devilish challenge. "Do you not know the way to Dallas?"

Del had just popped the top on his second diet cola of the day—and it wasn't even noon yet—when his front door burst open. Clint, Kat and Bull, the rangers of Company G, who sat around his kitchen table slurping colas of their own, all turned their heads as Elisa marched past them, Wal-Mart suitcase in hand and chin in the air.

For a moment, Del wondered if he was hallucinating.

The look she shot him as she passed proved he wasn't. It was as if the Abominable Snowman had frozen him with an icy breath. He couldn't remember a hallucination ever lowering the room temperature.

He pushed back from the table. "Elisa, what are you doing?"

He knew the moment Bull recognized her. His blue eyes turned to steel. Clint and Kat weren't far behind in catching on. Their mouths gaped.

Del's throat went dry. This was bad. Very, very bad.

Elisa dropped the suitcase. It landed beside her with a thud. "I'm looking for my husband. Who, it seems, would rather spend time with his ranger buddies than his wife on our honeymoon," she added sweetly.

"Wife!" Bull boomed. Del flinched.

Kat's gaze darted between him and Elisa. She pursed her lips. "Honeymoon?"

Del fired a look at Clint. "Well, do you want to get in a shot, too?"

Clint sipped his cola and clunked the can down on the table, implacable as ever. "Nope."

They didn't call him Cool-Hand Clint for nothing.

"What the hell's going on, Cooper?" Bull's voice was tight now, controlled, but his left hand crumpled his aluminum can as if it was paper. The last bit of suds dribbled over his fist unnoticed.

Del pulled in a deep breath, let it gust out. "Guys, there's something you should know."

They stared up at him expectantly, Clint with his look of practiced indifference, Kat, her eyes alight with anticipation like a kid at Christmas. And Bull. A lock of black hair had fallen over the captain's forehead, shadowing his eyes and lending an air of dangerous authority.

The silence crackled like a cheap radio.

With her typical lack of patience, Kat jumped up. "Oh, my God. It's true, isn't it? You two got married!"

Del didn't have to say yes. The fact that he didn't deny it was damning enough.

"Down, junior," Bull silenced Kat before she chattered on. Then he turned to Del. When he spoke, his lips hardly seemed to move. "We need to talk." His gaze skidded over to Elisa, then back. *"Outside."*

Del turned to follow his captain to the door, but pulled up short. He couldn't bring himself to walk past Elisa.

She stood before him in full Amazon princess mode. Her chin was high, her shoulders square. Her dark eyes glittered like the polished stones he'd called tiger's eye as a kid.

She looked noble and magnificent and yet somehow…exposed. He'd hurt her by leaving her last night, he realized, and the knowledge stung.

Bull glowered at him with his hand on the doorknob. "Are you coming?"

Del managed a small smile for Elisa. "No, sir," he said softly. "I believe my wife is the one I need to talk to right now."

Even Clint showed a moment's surprise at that. He shoved to his feet, motioned toward Kat. "Come on, kid. Let's make some space."

Bull pulled the door open for them.

"I'd appreciate it," Del said before the rangers made a hasty escape, "if this didn't make it into any official reports. At least for a while."

Clint acknowledged with a mock salute. Kat's blond curls bobbed when she stopped and, practically dancing on tiptoe, said, "You don't have to worry about me. And congratulations."

Clint nudged her out the door. "Get a clue, kid."

Del lost the rest of the lecture as Clint and Kat

tromped down the wooden stairs outside his door. Only Bull stayed. His eyes locked on Del's as if no one else existed. Del had seen that intensity make hardened criminals wet their pants.

He managed to limit his reaction to a mere shuffling of his feet.

The Bull loosened his grip on the doorknob. ''Always were a hard case when you had something stuck in your craw.''

''Some people would call that standing by my principles.''

''Some people would call it foolish.'' Fatigue—or concern?—stretched the skin tight across the captain's cheeks. ''You're risking everything. Your job. Your reputation.''

Del held his back upright through sheer will. The Cooper name had been held in honor by three generations— his grandfather, who'd landed at Normandy and lost a leg; his father, who'd given his life in a nameless jungle; and his brother, Sam, who had died for no reason other than sitting on the wrong side of the table at a sidewalk café.

Sam hadn't died in battle, but he'd been in uniform at the time, and in a foreign land. That made him a hero.

But some things were more important than a name. Paying a debt was one of them.

''Small price for a man's life, don't you think?'' he said, looking at Elisa, the barely perceptible bulge of her pregnancy beneath her loose blouse.

''You followed procedure to the letter,'' the captain countered. ''You can't blame yourself.''

''Apparently the shooting board does.'' The rangers

hadn't just happened by today. They'd come to commiserate about the bad news.

Bull growled an oath. "Pinheaded pencil pushers have never been in a firefight in their lives." He stepped over the threshold. Before he closed the door behind himself, he squared his jaw determinedly. "It isn't over with the shooting board yet, Del. Not if I have anything to say about it."

Del shoved his hands in his pockets and rattled change. "It won't be easy now."

They both knew why. She was standing between them.

"That's okay." Bull trailed a lingering look over Elisa, then beamed a blinding smile at them both. "Ain't no challenge in easy."

The moment they were alone, Elisa spun toward Del. Sometime during the previous five minutes, her outrage had faded. Now worry rumpled her soft face like a mussed blanket. "What did you mean, 'Apparently the shooting board does'?"

Del dropped into his easy chair and bunched his fists in eyes, then squinted up at Elisa. "How did you get here?"

"Your grandmother loaned me her pickup truck. What did you mean about the shooting board?"

Del lurched to his feet. His grandmother's pickup? There was a frightening thought. Elisa trying to navigate Central Expressway traffic. He paced passed her, trying not to notice how smooth her skin felt when he brushed her shoulder. "Do you even have a driver's license?"

She followed him. "I know how to drive."

"That's not what I asked." When he stopped suddenly, she bumped into his back. He turned and found her close enough to count each individual eyelash as they swept to her cheek and back up, robbing him of the argument he was about to make.

A blink. That's all it took from her to turn his brain into spaghetti.

Guilt. That had to be it. He looked at her and saw a woman in need. A woman alone because of him.

He saw his mother raising two boys while grieving over her dead husband, and slowly losing her mind in the process.

And he couldn't let that happen to Elisa.

She was strong, but she wasn't invincible. Looking at her was like looking at one of those hologram postcards. Most of the time, he saw his Amazon princess, stalwart and sturdy. But sometimes, when the light was just right, the way it had been when he'd found her in the cemetery chapel, and again after her sonogram, he saw a different Elisa.

In those rare moments, he saw the woman within the warrior. He saw her uncertainty in herself as a mother. He saw her worry over her baby's future and her own. He saw her loneliness, no one to share her burdens with.

He saw her vulnerability.

Looking up at him, she moistened her lips with the tip of her tongue.

Guilt. It was definitely guilt that made him want to drench them with his own.

Guilt, and a healthy dollop of lust.

"What happened with the shooting board?" she asked. Her breasts brushed his chest as she spoke.

He answered her as if through a haze, never consciously thinking about the words. His thoughts were all about her. The delicate shell of her ear parting the glossy curtain of hair on one side of her head. The tiny flecks of black inside her deep-brown irises. The scent of vanilla and almonds hovering around her like a karmic aura.

He inhaled, let her aroma fill him. It made his head light. He was floating, drifting up. The Rangers, the shooting board, everything he'd once considered important shrank to insignificant specs on a patchwork countryside far below him.

Everything except Elisa, that is.

She was with him. All around him. Inside him. Nothing else mattered. And because it didn't matter, he was able to say the words.

"The investigators filed a preliminary report finding me negligent in firing into the warehouse. I've been suspended from the Rangers without pay until the investigation is complete."

Chapter 8

Negligent? Suspended?

"This is not possible!" Elisa said, disbelieving what she'd heard. "You are *policía*. They cannot touch you."

"This is America, not San Ynez." The ranger's words seemed to come from a great distance. But the rest of him was close. Too close.

At this distance, she could feel the thump of his heart vibrating the air around them. Smell the soap he had washed with that morning.

See the smoke in his eyes.

He lifted a hand to her head, rubbed a lock of her hair between this thumb and fingers, testing its texture. "They can do a lot more than touch me," he said absently. His knuckles brushed her neck, setting off a string of microscopic explosions beneath her skin. "They can shove me right into the unemployment line."

"No." Even dogs did not turn on a member of their own pack.

"Yes." His gaze traveled down her body and back, and she felt his perusal like a brushstroke. The blood in her veins felt sparkly, as if it was filled with glitter. "At least if they fire me you won't have to worry about being married to a *policía* anymore."

The sweet warmth spreading inside her curdled. She knew what being a ranger meant to him. It was more than a job. It was a way to carry on a family tradition of service. It was a matter of honor.

Did he really believe she would be happy to see him lose what meant so much to him? Did she seem so callous to him?

She stepped back, put breathing room between them. "Is that what you think I'm worried about?"

The ranger angled himself away from her, spoke to her in profile. "You don't have to worry about anything at all. Whatever happens to me, my grandmother will make sure you're—"

The dismissive wave he aimed at her stirred up a gale of rage. "I did not marry your grandmother. I married *you*."

She stepped in front of him, and once again they stood breath to breath. The air between them roiled with the mix of her hot rage and his cold indifference.

This time when he touched her hair, he wasn't testing its texture. He twisted it around his fist. Elisa wasn't sure if he tugged or if she leaned into him willingly. She only knew their hearts beat one after the other, like links in a chain. "Is that why you came back here? To make sure I don't neglect my husbandly duties?"

Her lips mere inches from his, she bit off every word in warning. "Not unless you have another wife with whom to perform them."

Surprise winged across his face like a startled dove.

An Important Message from the Editors

Dear Reader,

Because you've chosen to read one of our fine romance novels, we'd like to say "thank you!" And, as a special way to thank you, we've selected two books from our Suspense and Adventure series — an exhilarating combination of Harlequin Intrigue and Silhouette Intimate Moments books — plus an exciting Mystery Gift, to send you absolutely FREE! You'll get one book from each of the 2 series in this collection, with absolutely no obligation.

Please enjoy them with our compliments...

Pam Powers

P.S. And because we value our customers, we've attached something extra inside...

Peel off Seal and Place Inside...

The Editor's "Thank You" Free Gifts Include:

- 1 Harlequin Intrigue® book!
- 1 Silhouette Intimate Moments® book!
- An exciting mystery gift!

PLACE FREE GIFT SEAL HERE

Yes I have placed my Editor's "Thank You" seal in the space provided above. Please send me 2 FREE books and a fabulous Mystery Gift. I understand I am under no obligation to purchase any books, as explained on the back and on the opposite page.

◀ DETACH AND MAIL CARD TODAY! ▼

389 HDL DU3G   189 HDL DU3Q

FIRST NAME   LAST NAME

ADDRESS

APT.#   CITY

STATE/PROV.   ZIP/POSTAL CODE   (H-SA-05/03)

Thank You!

The Harlequin Reader Service® — Here's how it works:

Accepting your 2 free books and gift places you under no obligation to buy anything. You may keep the books and gift and return the shipping statement marked "cancel." If you do not cancel, about a month later we'll send you 4 additional books from the Suspense and Adventure Collection, which includes 2 Harlequin Intrigue books and 2 Silhouette Intimate Moments books, and bill you just $15.96 in the U.S., or $18.96 in Canada, plus 25¢ shipping and handling per book. That's a total saving of over 10% off the cover price! You may cancel at any time, but if you choose to continue, every month we'll send you 4 more books from the Suspense and Adventure collection, which you may either purchase at the discount price or return to us and cancel your subscription.

*Terms and prices subject to change without notice. Sales tax applicable in N.Y. Canadian residents will be charged applicable provincial taxes and GST.

BUSINESS REPLY MAIL
FIRST-CLASS MAIL   PERMIT NO. 717-003   BUFFALO, NY

POSTAGE WILL BE PAID BY ADDRESSEE

HARLEQUIN READER SERVICE
3010 WALDEN AVE
PO BOX 1867
BUFFALO NY 14240-9952

NO POSTAGE
NECESSARY
IF MAILED
IN THE
UNITED STATES

She had recognized his attempt to close himself off from her. To drive her away, leaving only his pain to keep him company. Too well she knew the anger that burned under the whip of injustice. Too often she had felt its sting.

The ranger believed he had done the only thing he could, firing into the warehouse where Eduardo stood, unseen. Over the past week, she had come to believe it, too. He was not a careless man or one who took lightly the loss of life.

A breath shuddered out of him. Calm settled in his gray eyes. The storm had passed. For now.

"I make it a point never to have more than one wife around at a time." Gently he unwound his hand from her hair.

"But then, I am not a real wife, am I?"

"Felt pretty damn real yesterday."

The kiss. The sudden memory of it drew her gaze to his mouth. The sultry slant of his lips taunted her. So close, and yet so out of reach.

"Is that why you ran away?" she asked.

"Is that why you followed me?"

"No." The ranger was not the man she had planned to marry when she came to America. He was not the father of her child. He was simply a man, caught up by life just as she was, and struggling to maintain his honor in the face of a cruel circumstance. She could not, would not, think of him as more.

As a lover.

Eight years ago, Elisa had sworn to hold freedom above all else, relinquishing her independence neither for man nor state. She broke that vow when she married the ranger. For her baby's sake she sacrificed her pride, surrendered her dignity and consigned her future to the hands of a stranger.

She would not give him her heart, too.

Yet still she needed him—not just the name he had given her, but *him*. Their lives were bound together by a single, shattering moment that flung them both in a new direction. He was her rudder on this uncharted course.

She was alone except for him.

"Why, then?" he prodded. "Why did you come back?"

Elisa's reasons were clear to her. The words to explain them were not. Mami had been right. Marriage was intensely personal. But Elisa wasn't accustomed to exposing her innermost self. To trusting.

She lowered her eyes. "I have a doctor's appointment."

"Day after tomorrow. I haven't forgotten. I would have come for you."

"Do you want me to leave?"

"No." His gaze flicked aside like a child kicking a stone in frustration. "I just want to know why you're here. God damn it—"

She frowned fiercely.

"Sorry." He pulled in a deep breath and stared at her so intensely she thought she might melt. "I just want to know where we stand."

He was giving her a chance, she recognized. A portal through which she could pull him closer or shut him off from her entirely. She wished she had the courage to choose one side or the other, but she did not. The best she could manage was to straddle the line.

Shoulders trembling ever so slightly, she lifted her chin. "We have an agreement. We stand on either side of it."

"My baby has grown?"

Turning away from the computer screen displaying Elisa's sonogram, Dr. Marsala's large nose bobbed. She smiled. "Right through the minimum range and edging up on the median size for her gestational age."

A cool wash of tears flooded Elisa's eyes. She made the sign of the cross over herself and said a quick prayer of thanks before she realized what the doctor had said.

"Her?"

The doctor's smile broadened. "You said you wanted to know if I was sure, and I'm sure. This little one doesn't have the right plumbing to be a boy. You're having a little girl."

"A girl!" Elisa's heart swelled. She had been so sure it would be a boy, with dark hair and eyes, and sharp features like his father. But this time when she closed her eyes, it was a girl child she saw, with the Ranger's gray eyes.

She nearly started off the table.

"Something wrong?" Dr. Marsala asked, switching off the computer.

"No." She sat up, still distracted by the image of Del Cooper's daughter. A daughter she would never bear him. "I am fine. I just…was sure it was a boy."

The doctor bent over a file folder, making notes. "Well, after she's born, you can trade her in if you don't like her."

Shock tied Elisa's tongue for a full second before she realized the doctor was joking.

Ten minutes later Elisa burst through the door. The Ranger sat in a corner, his long body crammed into a too-small chair in the empty waiting room. He was reading a magazine on parenting.

When he raised his head, the hollow look in his eyes stopped Elisa cold. She had never seen him afraid before.

For her? Of the news?

Swallowing a lump of gratitude for his concern, she hurried toward him. He stood, and she was on him before she thought her actions through and stopped herself.

Her arms closed around his neck and she buried her face in his shoulder, chattering in Spanish one long, run-on sentence that probably made no sense.

Apparently he understood at least two words: *baby* and *okay.*

His arms around the small of her back, he gathered her up, awkwardly at first. Tentatively. Then with gusto. "I told you everything would be all right."

"You didn't know."

"Did so."

"Did not."

Gently, he lifted her off her feet, balancing her on his chest. "Did—"

Grinning, she punched him in the arm.

"If this is how you two celebrate, I'd hate to see you fight." Hands in the pockets, the doctor swished the hem of her lab coat around her thighs.

The Ranger set Elisa on her feet and extended his hand. "Thanks for everything, doc."

"You're quite welcome," she said, then handed Elisa a prescription. "This is for your new prenates. Everything is looking great, but I'd like to see you again in ten days or so, just to check your progress."

With one arm around her waist, the Ranger pulled Elisa against his hip. "We'll be here."

"Good. And one more thing." The doctor smiled at each of them. "You can consider this your green light."

"Green light?" Elisa crinkled her nose and looked at the Ranger for explanation. Her vocabulary was extensive, but idioms—which she assumed this was, since there were no traffic control signals in the doctor's waiting room—sometimes escaped her.

Was he blushing? Something certainly had his cheeks abloom.

"I think the doctor means it's okay to, ah…"

Understanding unfurled in her, warm and deep. "Oh. We're not—"

He silenced her with a squeeze and made a hasty goodbye.

Outside she pulled out of his grasp. Nonplussed, he strode on to the Land Rover.

"What was that about?" she asked, two steps behind him. "You didn't have to let her think—"

"We're supposed to be married."

"We *are* married."

"Married people have sex."

She almost bumped into his back when they reached the car. "We're not that married," she said dryly, though she knew he was right. If she was to stay in the United States, they needed their marriage to look real. That meant keeping the fact that they were not intimate to themselves.

He unlocked the passenger door, opened it for her. On the seat inside, a package waited like a found penny.

"For me?" she guessed, touched.

He nodded. "A little celebration."

"How did you know…? Wh-what if the news—"

He lifted a finger to her lips. "Sshh. Not a chance." He shrugged guiltily. "Besides, I checked with the nurse before I ran down here and put it in. Barely got back upstairs before you were done.''

A well of fear she had carried so deep inside her that she hadn't realized it was there opened up. Hope rushed in, and tears of joy and relief rose inside her.

She lifted the rectangular package as if it were fragile as a baby bird, turned it over in her hands. ''You wrapped it in pink,'' she said in awe.

''I knew it was a girl.''

''Did not.''

''Did so.''

''Not.'' She sniffed and punched him in the shoulder before she ripped open the pastel wrapping paper.

Frowning, he shuffled his feet while speechless, she stared at her present.

''It's a book,'' he said, sounding anxious over reaction.

''A book of baby names.'' Her voice wobbled. It just might be the most thoughtful gift she had ever received.

''I put sticky notes by my favorites.'' He leaned over her and thumbed through the pages. ''Here. Elena. Marianna. What about Xoria?''

He smiled. ''Okay. Maybe not Xoria.''

''Maybe not,'' she said, and impulsively kissed him on the cheek before she slid past him and into the Land Rover.

One corner of his mouth hitched up. ''Well, if that's the reward for a book.'' He reached into his pocket and pulled out two stubs of heavy paper. ''What're a couple of tickets behind home plate worth?''

Rolling her eyes at him, Elisa tipped the ranger back with one finger and closed the car door. Then, thinking better of herself, she pressed the button to lower the automatic window, reached out and snatched the tickets from his hand.

A little harmless flirtation was no reason to miss out on a baseball game.

The Rangers got slaughtered—the Texas Rangers Major League Baseball team, that is. After a three-up, three-down inning in the bottom of the sixth, the crowd at The Ballpark in Arlington began to thin.

By the time the ninth inning rolled around, clouds covered the moon and a warm mist perfumed the air with the scent of summer rain. Only the most die-hard fans remained, Elisa among them.

Del had never seen her so animated. While she'd followed every pitch enthusiastically, he'd been more interested in watching her.

Her eyes were alight with laughter. Her voice rang clear and true with her cheers and jeers. Excitement flushed her cheeks each time a runner slid to his base or a fly ball soared toward the outfield wall. And no matter which team scored or struck out, a California brownout couldn't have dimmed her smile.

He supposed she had a lot to be happy about today.

That made one of them, at least.

He just wished the news he'd gotten from a call to Captain Matheson had been as reassuring as her doctor's visit. The Bull had spoken again to the investigators on his case but wasn't convinced it had done any good.

Like the Texas Ranger at the plate now, Del's career was down, no balls, two strikes, with two out in the bottom of the ninth.

Elisa jumped to her feet, bobbed like a pogo stick, clapping, when the Texas batter took his final swing and met nothing but air. "We won! We won!"

"You could be a little less enthusiastic about it," Del grumbled, suppressing a smile. Even her insistence on rooting for the Minnesota Twins charmed him.

A light rain began to fall as they left the stadium. Fat, warm droplets splattered on concrete only to be slurped away by the thirsty landscape. Del laced his fingers with Elisa's and pulled her to him, sheltering her as much as he could with his body. She didn't seem to mind, so he nudged her closer to his side and an inch or two in front of him so that the outer slope of her breast rested on his rib cage and the curve of her backside brushed his thigh with each step they took.

In a moment of pure indulgence, Del wished he had parked farther away. Holding her this way felt good. It soothed an ache.

Soothed, hell. She turned her head up to smile at him, and the glimpse of wet T-shirt stretched over firm, female breasts nearly buckled his knees.

His body tightened. Blood flowed downward, concentrated.

Del cursed himself. Despite a concerted mental effort, he couldn't stop it. And in a pair of wet Levi's, it wasn't going to be easy to hide it.

He needed a distraction.

"Did you see Carter's arm on the mound?" Elisa asked, still staring up at him, still smiling. Still unaware.

He hoped.

"The Cowboys couldn't have hit him tonight if he'd been throwing beach balls," she finished.

"Rangers," he said. "Cowboys are football."

"Cowboys, Rangers, whatever. It is confusing, is it not, calling them the same as the police?" She scrunched her nose. "Why did you name yourselves after a baseball team, anyway?"

"I think it was the other way aroun—" he started before he realized she was baiting him. And had caught him, hook, line and sinker, as the saying went.

"Get in," he said, shaking his head at her cheeky grin. Who'd have thought the girl could go from noblewoman to royal imp in just one day? At least the banter took his mind off his...discomfort.

Until he climbed into the Rover next to her.

The dome light threw the shadows of a thousand tiny goose bumps down her arms.

"You're cold," he accused as if it was a felony.

"Just excited." She crossed her arms and rubbed, but the motion plumped her breasts together. Her arms weren't the only parts of her that had pebbled. Two perfect, pert peaks pointed at him from beneath the damp, clingy cotton of her shirt.

"It was a great game, no?"

"Yeah, sure," he said, even though he couldn't remember who had been playing, with her looking at him like that.

"The Rangers made a good show."

Now he remembered. Sort of. "They got trounced twelve to two."

"They...tried hard."

Hard was not a word he needed to hear right now. "Maybe one of these days we'll get a pitcher, and you can see a real game," he grumbled.

She threw her head back against the seat, smile blazing. "I still had a great time."

He barely acknowledged what she said. Barely heard it.

This was not good. If he didn't pull himself together, he was going to embarrass them both and ruin a great evening. The first really comfortable evening they'd spent together.

Moving gingerly, guarding against the pinch of tight, wet denim on sensitive flesh, he leaned behind the passenger seat, opened the gym bag he kept there and pulled out a towel.

"Here," he gruffed, resolutely holding his gaze above her neckline. "Don't want to catch a chill."

She wiped her face on the terry cloth, then ran it down the length of each arm, circled her delicate wrists, and brought one corner up to her neck. Mesmerized, he couldn't have cut his gaze away with a chainsaw as she dipped the corner beneath the collar of her shirt and down, down into that sweet, dark valley in the center of her chest, triggering a string of explosions in Del's groin.

How the hell was he going to live with this woman for two years? He was going to lose his mind. Or the motor function in his lower extremities. Could a man even survive a two-year hard-on?

He had a feeling he was going to find out.

Elisa curved one arm behind her head and swept her hair forward, over her shoulder, to towel it off. She missed a few strands.

"Here, let me," he heard himself saying, and took the towel from her. He pulled her hair together, wrapped it in cotton and began fingering it dry.

"You have great hair." Long, straight and glossy, it cascaded down her back like a sable waterfall. He wanted to tangle his hands in it, bind their bodies together with it while they rolled together, naked on a big, soft bed.

But tonight he'd settle for getting it dry.

"Thank you," she said, a bit shyly. Had she heard more in his voice than a simple compliment?

He raised the towel to her head and massaged gently. His fingers probed slow, deep circles around her temples first, and then at the sides of her head, behind her ears.

"And thank you for tonight," she added. "It was very special."

"I'm glad you had a good time." He moved his hands lower, pulling the towel along, to a spot just above her nape and dug deep into her muscles with his thumbs. A tiny moan escaped her, and he thought he might have pressed too hard until she pushed back into his touch.

"Mmm, that feels good."

The towel fell away, and there was just his hands in her silky hair. On her silky skin.

He leaned close to her ear. "'Lisa?"

"Mmm?" Her eyes were closed. Her lips parted.

"Do you want me to make it feel even better?"

She shifted her head toward him until their noses bumped. Her eyes were dark and heavy. Her lips were just a breath away from his.

"Yes," she whispered, and he had no doubt she knew what he'd been asking.

So simple. No hysterics. No coy denials. Just pure, honest need.

He kissed her the same way. Lightly at first, nuzzling and getting to know the shape and taste of her. Letting her get used to the shape and taste of him. He didn't want this to explode with the kind of flash-grenade intensity that had overcome them after the wedding. He wanted to learn what she liked, show her what he liked. He wanted it to build slowly. Unbearably.

Rain splattered on the windshield. A jet cruised low overhead on its way into D/FW airport. The rumble of its engines vibrated through the Land Rover. Outside, the

crunch of gravel marked the steps of another fan who'd
held out to the last pitch.

All of it was lost in a pool of greater sensation. Elisa's
lips fusing to his. The dance of her slender tongue. Her
hands fisted in his hair.

With one arm behind her back he lifted her to him.
She arched, and the peaks that had intrigued him earlier
scraped across his chest, making him grab for a breath
like a drowning man.

With his free hand he felt for her, found the soft
mound and the hardened tip. His thumb streaked across
the cool dampness of her shirt until the warmth of the
flesh beneath soaked through.

A breath shuddered out of her. He ducked his head to
her throat, nipped at the vein that jumped to greet him.
She jolted.

Damn, she was responsive. Her hands were everywhere. On his head, his neck, his chest, pushing.

"Del."

Pushing? Of course. He should have known better.
She didn't want him. It was wrong, sick for him to want
her. The woman who should have married another man.
A man he'd killed.

"Del!"

Stomach coiling, he raised his head and found her staring toward him with wide, startled eyes. It took a moment for his sex-fogged mind to realize the look wasn't
for him, but for something beyond.

He spun in his seat, instinctively pushing Elisa behind
him, and squinted through the dimples of rain on the
window.

Outside, a man wearing a black trench coat and a ball
cap with no insignia squinted back.

Chapter 9

Elisa slammed her fist down on the door lock button.

Her lips were still tender from the ranger's kisses, her breasts felt full and pendulous from his caresses, and her breathing had yet to find an even pace, but her defenses were on full alert.

She had lived too long in San Ynez not to sense a clear and present danger.

Studying the man outside, she coiled her legs beneath her, ready to spring.

The ranger wiped the condensation from the window and thudded the glass with the heel of his hand. ''Hey, buddy, you wanna watch some action, rent a videotape!''

But the voyeur wasn't put off. He just stared at them. Or rather at *her*.

Cold fingers danced up her spine.

The ranger reached for the window control. ''Did you hear—''

''No.'' She captured his wrist before he lowered the

glass. "Let us go. Please," she implored when he made no move to start the car.

The ranger scowled at her a long moment, but he turned the key in the ignition. As they drove off, he craned his head, studying the man for as long as he could see him, no doubt trying to memorize the intruder's features so he could match them to mug shots later.

Only, if Elisa was right, there wouldn't be any mug shots.

"You want to tell me what that was about?" the ranger asked grimly as they pulled onto Highway 183.

"Before that man showed up or after?" She had a bad feeling about the stranger's presence, but she didn't want to discuss it with a Texas Ranger. It involved too many aspects of her life that she would rather not have American law enforcement know about.

"After." The ranger's fingers flexed on the leather steering wheel cover. His voice softened. He took his eyes off the road long enough to ignite her. "Let's save the other conversation for later, okay? When we both have a little…perspective."

She shrugged, covering her relief. She was not sure she would ever have perspective enough to rationally discuss what had passed between them. Her marriage to the ranger might not be real, but her desire for him was.

"Did you know that man?" the ranger persisted.

"No."

"You were in an awful hurry to get out of there."

She picked at her seat belt. "You are not carrying your gun since you were suspended, and we were alone there."

"What makes you think I need a gun against some freak who gets his jollies watching people make out."

Heat flashed in her cheeks, but she pushed the flames

back. "You are a police officer. Do you really think he was just a random voyeur?"

"Do you have reason to believe otherwise?"

"His clothes were expensive. His trousers were pressed. He stood straight, not slouching, and he did not react, either backing down or showing aggression when you challenged him."

He glanced at her again, his eyes narrow. "You don't miss much, do you?"

"I can't afford to." They turned off the highway, and she checked the sideview mirror for the third time in as many miles. She took some comfort in the knowledge that the ranger had done the same twice as often.

"There's no one back there." He studied her a moment, then asked, "Elisa, are you sure you don't know that man?"

"No," she admitted. "But I know his type. He is someone's watchdog."

"Whose?"

She shook her head. She had said too much.

He whipped the car into the parking lot of a convenience store and shoved the transmission into park. Flashing neon signs that read ATM, Money Orders and Cappuccino beckoned her inside, but gunmetal-gray eyes pinned her in her seat.

"If you're in trouble, Elisa, you have to tell me. I can protect you."

But would he? She had seen the values he lived by: God, country and the Texas Rangers. Not necessarily in that order.

She shook her head, her lips clamped together and his taste still lingering on them.

"You are in trouble, aren't you?" His face twisted.

"And you'd rather endanger your child than tell me what the hell is going on? Who is following you?"

"I do not know."

"Who do you *think* is following you?"

Her hands fisted, a seed of anger planted in her by a nameless face in the dark. "Your government?" she suggested. "Mine?"

"The United States Government doesn't send goons out to spy on every alien who crosses the border. Why would they be interested in you?"

Elisa had believed she could live with the ranger, accept his protection from the INS without telling him the whole truth about herself.

She had been a fool.

Now that the time for full disclosure had come, she found it more difficult than she had ever imagined. Because his opinion mattered now, she realized. He was not the heartless automaton, the hired gun she had once thought him to be. And, realizing that, she feared the truth would cause her to lose everything she had gained in the past week: the fragile friendship between them; the grudging respect; the passion that had burned so brightly but so briefly.

All would be lost to her before the night was out.

"Because your government stands by and does nothing while the illegal regime currently in power in San Ynez enslaves its people and rapes its economy," she said, meeting his gaze levelly, if sadly. "*I* do not."

"You're a *rebel?*" Even the word tasted bad to Del.

Elisa slanted her chin. "I am a member of the People's Resistance Party. We are freedom fighters."

All the air inside the Land Rover vanished. Del couldn't breathe. Strangling, he shoved the door open and jumped out. In contradiction to his roiling emotions, the night was calm. The rain had stopped. Crickets chirped in the pasture next to the gas station. The smell of fresh-cut hay mingled with the tang of gasoline from the pumps. Del leaned against the quarter panel of his car and breathed it in.

Elisa, a rebel. He should have known it the minute she jumped him behind that warehouse. She fought like a pro. Then there was her story about Eduardo. She'd met him when the soldiers attacked. All the signs had been there. He just hadn't seen them. Hadn't wanted to see them.

He'd been too busy looking at her fine hair and perfect breasts.

He turned, leaned over his forearms on the hood and gave his steel-belted Michelin a swift kick.

God, he didn't understand people like her. Men and women without conscience who made war on their own governments—and anyone else who got in their way—in the name of God, politics or profit.

Now he'd married one of them. Promised to protect her.

How the hell was he supposed to live with that?

When he lifted his head, she stood beside him. He hadn't even heard her approach. If she'd had a knife, she could have planted it in his back already.

He considered himself lucky for a moment, then cursed himself for thinking it. Fifteen minutes ago he'd been hot for this woman. She hadn't changed since then. He was the one who was different.

"I told you my brother, Sam, died in Saudi Arabia," he said by way of explanation. "I didn't tell you how."

She waited in silence while he gathered his thoughts.

Separated the words from the emotion so that he could speak them.

"We both had passes off the base. I wanted to go into the city, see the sights, soak up a little culture. I had one of those disposable cameras, and I had this stupid idea about getting our pictures taken on camels…"

He swallowed hard before he could continue. "Sam didn't really want to go, but did. Said somebody had to keep me out of trouble. We stopped for lunch at this little sidewalk café. Sam took the seat closer to the street." His face twisted. "You never think about it, you know? How an insignificant decision like which chair you take at a table can mean the difference between life and death.

"We were almost finished eating when a truck pulled up to the curb. All I remember is a roar and a blast of heat. Dust and pebbles stinging my skin. I yelled for Sam, but everybody was screaming, and I didn't hear him answer, so I crawled around. I cut my hands and my knees on all the broken glass, but I didn't even feel it at the time. I didn't feel anything until I realized I was crawling in something pasty. I looked down, and realized it was blood. Sam's blood."

Elisa filled the long silence that followed. "I am sorry."

"The suicide bomber killed eight people that day, including a five-year-old girl and a sixty-eight-year-old woman. About a week later some left-wing political group no one had even heard of took credit.

"That's why I quit the army and became a ranger, 'Lis. To make sure that kind of insane, senseless violence never happens in my country."

"And now here I am."

"Here you are."

"I am sorry for what you have suffered. But are you so sure of yourself, Ranger?" Her voice was hypnotic. It called him to listen. To trust, even when he didn't want to. "Has your loss made you a champion of justice? Or blind to injustice, even where it is real and grave?"

"I don't know," he admitted, shaking his head. "All I know is that I would give my life for my country if need be."

"Would you kill for it, as well?"

"I would." He gritted his teeth. "I have. But I haven't slaughtered civilians in the streets because I don't agree with their politics."

"And neither have I. Mine is a peaceful cause. We are outnumbered and outgunned. We fight only as a last resort, when we are attacked and there is nowhere to run and no place to hide."

"That's not what the news reports say."

"Propaganda, created by Colonel Sanchez, the leader of the military regime that took power after they murdered Presidente Herrerra, to gain the sympathy of American policymakers."

"President Herrerra died in a boating accident."

"Yes. His yacht was accidentally torpedoed by Colonel Sanchez's navy."

Del straightened. Studied her doubtfully. She made it sound plausible, if not probable.

"Sanchez put a stranglehold on the country," she said. "He closed the schools and seized the hospitals."

"There was rioting in the streets. Looting."

"Soldiers masquerading as civilians so the people would not resist when military law was instituted. Then he brought in the cocaine growers and turned the tourist resorts into terrorist training camps."

"While the rest of the world was blissfully unaware."

"Visas for foreign journalists were revoked. The San Ynezian broadcasters only dared air the reports he provided."

Elisa stepped closer. Her eyes were bright with a different kind of passion than he'd seen earlier tonight. A passion for principle. "You know where I was during all this? I was a graduate student in International Marketing and Business Law at San Ynez University. I thought my purpose in life was to help my country become part of the worldwide marketplace. I wanted to bring new opportunities to my people. New ways of thinking."

Her expression saddened. "One day I was lecturing on the North American Free Trade Agreement to an assembly of undergrads when a group of soldiers burst in. They said they were closing the university and we were ordered to disperse.

"Some of the students shouted at the soldiers. Someone started pushing. Then there were screams. I was at the microphone. I asked everyone to calm down, to do as they were told, but a fight broke out." Elisa's bright eyes turned glassy. "The soldiers fired into the crowd. Three of my students were killed. I held one of them, a young man named Guillermo, while he died. Then I was taken away."

"Away where?" Del didn't want to ask, couldn't stand not to.

"My younger brothers and I were incarcerated in the presidential palace and interrogated as dissidents for three days before we finally escaped. Soon after, the resistance party was founded, and I had a new purpose in life."

Would he have done differently? Who was to say?

Love of country ran deep in his veins, a legacy passed

to him from his father and grandfather. But what would he do if the country itself became cancerous? If a disease infected the government from within?

The questions whirled in his mind until he was dizzy. There was no sense agonizing about a future that would, in all probability, never happen.

Nor about a past he couldn't change.

Elisa was what she was. It didn't negate his debt to her, or his promises.

"What about now, Elisa?" he asked. "What's your purpose now?"

She smoothed her palm over the small bulge just below her waistline. "Now I have a child to consider, and nothing matters except keeping her safe."

That, at least, they could agree on. "Then let's get the two of you home."

In the hours before dawn, Del punched the couch cushions and tried to find a spot more comfortable than the last 220 he had tried.

It was no use. Sleep was a wish upon a star tonight.

He got up, pulled his laptop from the desk drawer in the corner and booted up the machine. He still hadn't been able to reconcile the Elisa he knew with his image of a third-world rebel. She was too intelligent, too ethical, too…vulnerable.

But the farther he traveled on the tangled strands of the World Wide Web, the more believable her story became. Reports of former Presidente Herrerra's "boating accident" were sketchy at best. All the reliable foreign news sources had gradually left or been driven out of San Ynez, and the local reports read like campaign flyers. Anonymous Web sites, complete with photos that might or might not have been real, documenting human rights atrocities in the country dotted the Internet.

The one thing missing was an official U.S. position on the happenings. The greatest advocate of peace and democracy on Earth had been conspicuously silent on the subject of San Ynez.

Interesting.

Straightening his tie, Del stopped outside the door to the offices of Texas Rangers Company G and pretended his stomach wasn't about to turn itself inside out.

The morning had been hell. He and Elisa had tiptoed around each other like worms at a pro fishermen's convention.

"You go ahead," he'd said, standing outside the bathroom door.

"No, you first."

"It's okay. You go."

"After you."

Then the call from Captain Matheson had come in. Del was wanted at the office. The Bull hadn't been told why, and he wasn't happy about it.

At precisely fifteen seconds before nine o'clock, the time he'd been ordered to report, he pulled open the door to conference room J-12. To his great surprise, there were no DPS investigators inside.

To his even greater surprise, the director of the Texas Rangers himself, the honorable J. William Peters, commanded the head of the table. Del had never seen the man in Dallas before. When J. William wanted to see a ranger, he snapped his fingers and the ranger got himself to Ranger headquarters in Austin, pronto. If J. William was here, the news couldn't be good.

"Sit. I understand you've been briefed on the shoot

team's preliminary findings,'' the director said, flipping pages in a folder on the table.

Del scraped a chair back and lowered himself into it, fighting back anger and to his horror, moisture in his eyes. He'd done the only thing he could at the warehouse, damn it. And an innocent man had died because of it. ''Yes, sir, I've seen the report. And I respectfully conclude it is a bunch of bunk. Sir.''

''Del.'' He looked up from his folder. ''I can call you Del, can't I? We're informal here.''

''Sure. As long as I can call you J. William.''

Director Peters closed the folder. ''Sarcasm is not going to help you, Ranger Cooper. I'm sure you know there is a lot to be considered in this investigation. The public is outraged at the death—''

''I wasn't aware the public conducted internal DPS investigations, sir.''

''And I wasn't aware you had such a disrespectful mouth.''

''Sir, it's just that—''

The director waved him off. ''Forget it, Cooper. I'm here on another matter, anyway.'' Before Del asked what matter, Peters folded his hands into a spire atop Del's case folder. ''It's come to my attention that you married recently.''

Del's blood ran cold. How the hell had he found out about that? It was a sure bet no one in Company G had told him.

''And that your new…wife…is involved in this case.''

''She's been cleared of any wrongdoing, sir. She was just in the wrong place.''

''I believe she was in the right place—paying a visit to her previous fiancé, if I'm not mistaken. The man you killed, Eduardo Garcia. A man who also happens to be the father of her child."

Del didn't think confirmation was necessary.

"I'm sure you can see how puzzling your sudden marriage appears, Ranger. One might even say it doesn't seem real."

Damn, damn, damn. "The license was properly applied for, sir, and the ceremony legally noted."

The director kicked back in his chair and clunked a snakeskin boot onto the table. "But do you love each other?"

Del's jaw tightened. He couldn't say yes. He wasn't a liar. But he wasn't the kind of man to go back on his promises, either, and if he said no, he could kiss Elisa goodbye. She would be deported.

"Elisa and I share a strong bond," he finally said, hedging as best he could. "Beyond that, our relationship is private."

"Let's be blunt, son." The director leaned forward. "Did you marry the girl to keep her in the country, or just because she's got a nice ass?"

Del's chair clattered over backward. On his feet, he swiped his Stetson from the table and headed for the door.

"I'm sure you can see how badly your marriage could reflect on this organization, Cooper. One of our own attempting to defraud the INS. Some might even say you were trying to influence a witness."

"There is nothing for me to influence. My wife has no information with any bearing on the case."

"Let her go, boy. It's not too late to undo what you've done."

Well past his tolerance limit, Del spun toward the director. "Is that an order?"

''It's a choice. Let her go, or I'll have to let you go.''

A choice? His job or his wife? Break the vow he made at his wedding or the vow he made when he was sworn in as a Texas Ranger?

The decision should have been difficult. An unsolvable conundrum. But all he had to do was picture Elisa, holding Eduardo's body in her arms, to realize he had no choice at all.

There had been rangers before him and there would be rangers when he was gone.

There was only one Elisa.

Hands steadier than he'd imagined they would be, he released the catch on the silver circle and star pinned over his heart and tossed the Texas Ranger emblem on the table next to the director's boot heel.

J. William Peters kicked the badge off the edge of the table and into his hand. ''Delgado Cooper, your employment as a Texas Ranger is hereby terminated.''

Chapter 10

Del didn't wait to be dismissed by the director. Why bother with protocol? He wasn't a Texas Ranger anymore.

He'd been thrown out. Disgraced.

His face warmed and softened until it felt mushy. His throat shrank. Something cracked inside him, and shame oozed from the fissure.

Laughter tumbled down the hall to him. The dispatcher telling water-cooler jokes on her break again, probably.

He swiped the back of his hand across his eyes. He was not going to let them see him like this. He was not going to fall apart.

He turned the corner out of the break room. The sunshine pouring through the outside door at the end of the hall beckoned like the proverbial light at the end of the tunnel. Then the train hit him.

Captain Matheson stepped out of his office and caught

Del by the shoulder. The look in the Bull's eyes told Del he didn't need to brief his boss—former boss—on the latest turn of events.

"Cooper, I want you to know I didn't—"

"Forget it, I know." Del brushed him off and tried to pass, but Bull hooked his elbow.

"Come on," he nodded into his office. "Sit down. I'll buy you a cup of bad coffee."

Del couldn't do this. Couldn't dissect the end of his career, or talk about his feelings, or whatever the hell the captain wanted him to do. The wound was too fresh. Too deep. "Another time."

He tried to pull loose, but the captain's grip held. It was Del's temper that snapped. He brought his free arm around, latched his hand in Bull's collar and shoved him back. "Damn it, I said not now!"

The pity in Bull's eyes piqued both Del's anger and his shame. His heart felt as if it was trying to beat out of his chest and being ripped in two at the same time. He wanted to say something to the captain, something to let him know he was sorry, but he couldn't find the words.

He struck out for the door again, but Clint and Kat beat him to it. They were just coming in, blocking his way.

"Hey, Coop," Kat said, her perfect smile on high wattage. "What're you do—"

"Leaving, if you'd get the hell out of my way." Shouldering past his former partners, he slapped the bar that opened the door so hard the glass rattled.

The heat rising from the pavement outside felt good on his clammy skin. The blinding sun helped dry his eyes. He stood for a moment, soaking in the sights and sounds of the city he'd spent the greater part of his adult life protecting from harm.

He angled his head up to look at the green glass spire of the Bank One Building, the ball atop Reunion Tower. "You're on your own now, guys," he said.

"How sentimental," a man seated on a stone bench in the grass said. The speaker's back was to Del, but when he rose and turned, Del recognized Mr. Baseball—without the trench coat. Today he wore a charcoal business suit with a blue-and-red-striped tie.

The man crushed out a cigarette with his heel and strolled toward Del as if they were old friends.

"Who the hell are you?" Del's fingers itched for the Heckler and Koch .45 he'd left lying in the top drawer of his dresser.

"Call me a concerned citizen. Someone who believes in the same things you do. Which is why I hate to see you throwing your life away for someone who doesn't."

"Who would that be?"

"Your wife."

Now this was getting good. The man was talking himself right into a fight, and Del was just looking for something to break.

Casually he positioned himself on the opposite side of the man, putting the sun at his own back—and in his opponent's eyes. "How would you know what my wife believes in?"

"I know a good deal about Elisa Reyes. Perhaps more than you."

"Why don't you enlighten me?" Del wanted to hear what he had to say before he busted the man's face.

"She is a member of a revolutionary faction in San Ynez."

"Good guess. Now tell me something I don't know."

"How about the real reason she came to the United States?" The man pulled a folded square of paper from his breast pocket, opened it and handed it to Del. "Do you recognize that man?"

Del studied the grainy head shot, and the name and personal data below it. According to the sheet, he was Guillermo Santiago, of San Ynez.

He was also the man who had pointed a rifle at Clint Hayes from inside the warehouse, and who Del had killed to protect his fellow ranger, unknowingly hitting Eduardo Garcia as well.

"The gun buyer," Del said.

"That man is a member of the same revolutionary faction."

Del looked at the picture again, then back at the man who had given it to him. He knew what the man was implying—that Elisa had been part of the interrupted gun deal. He didn't believe it. Couldn't. And yet his heart sat in his chest like a lump of ice. "You got any proof, or you expect me to believe this fairy tale on your say-so?"

"I have nothing to prove to you, Mr. Cooper."

"No? Then what are you doing here?"

"Trying to convince you to cooperate, for your own sake."

"I'm not in a very cooperative mood right now."

"Let her go. Dissolve your marriage and send her home before you end up on the short end of the stick on this thing."

Del laughed harshly. "Too late."

"You think losing your job is the worst that can happen to you?"

How the hell did he know that already?

"Think again," the man continued. "Think about the term *negligent homicide*. Think about prison time. And while you're at it, think about me scaring up a few of poor Eduardo Garcia's long-lost relatives to file a civil suit for wrongful death. I understand your family owns a farm in Van Zandt county. It'd be a shame if they had to sell it to pay your court judgments.''

''Son of a bitch. Who are you?''

''With one phone call I can have the shooting board's final report in my hands.'' He paused just long enough to make it clear the report would say exactly what he wanted it to say, too. ''Five minutes after that, I'll have an arrest warrant made out in your name. I'll give you twenty-four hours to change your mind. At twenty-four-oh-one you'll be a wanted man.''

Del was stunned speechless.

''Things can get worse, Mr. Cooper,'' he said as he turned and strolled away. ''Things can always get worse.''

''You're scaring me.'' Del had been with Elisa, and yet not with her, all afternoon. She had seen others with the same distant look in their eyes, villagers whose homes had been shelled by the soldiers. They stumbled around in the rubble for hours, sometimes days, sifting through the broken shards of what used to be their lives.

But what had caused the ranger to feel as though his world had been destroyed, Elisa did not know. He had been this way since he came back from his meeting, but he would not tell her what happened. She knew only that he had pulled her from a pile of baby wallpaper samples and paint chips, insisting she help him run a few errands.

So far they had visited his insurance agent to have her listed as beneficiary on his policies, his bank to add her name to his accounts, his lawyer to draw up power of attorney for her and to change his will. Now he wanted to take her to apply for a driver's license.

He helped her into the Land Rover. "Just a few more stops, I promise."

"I am tired."

"You need to be able to get around town without depending on me."

"I am sorry to be such a burden to you," she snapped. She was not a nice person when she was tired, and these past few weeks she had not been able to function beyond 3:00 p.m. without a nap. It was now a quarter to four. "But do you think this could wait until tomorrow? I do not think I will score well on the driving test if I fall asleep behind the wheel."

Del braced himself against the top of the car. For a moment she almost thought he was going to insist she get her license today. "All right," he said, then sighed and shook his head. "You're right. You're supposed to be taking it easy."

He made it no easier to rest at home, though. He stalked from room to room, showing her where to find spare keys, bank statements, vehicle maintenance records. Finally she settled onto the couch and refused to move another inch. Del disappeared into the bedroom. When he returned, he held a pistol.

"I assume you know how to use one of these," he said, and she tried not to read any accusation into the words. The propensity for violence he assumed her to have was still a sore subject between them.

"Fifteen-round semiautomatic, thumb safety, barrel sights," she said. Her brothers had insisted she learn to shoot, though she never carried a weapon. Didn't own one. "I think I can manage."

"Good." He slammed a loaded magazine into the grip

and pulled the slide back to inject a round into the chamber before handing her the gun. "Take this until I get back."

"Where are you going?"

"To finish those errands."

"I am supposed to sit here with a gun under my pillow while you go buy groceries?"

"I'd rather you kept it out, where you can get to it faster." He picked up his keys from the coffee table. "And we have plenty of groceries."

"Then where are you going?"

"To rattle some bushes and see what jumps out."

"Bushes...?" Elisa shook her head, confused by the mental image she created from the literal translation of his words.

He paused at the front door and must have recognized her bewilderment. "I'm going to see what I can find out about our visitor at the ballpark last night."

Now Elisa was really worried. She had a bad feeling about this. "Why? Has something happened?"

The way he shifted his gaze told her it had—and that he didn't want to talk about it. He shook the doorknob. "Lock this when I leave. Don't let anyone in but me."

She opened her mouth to argue but changed her mind. Some problems had to be worked out on one's own. She had a feeling whatever was bothering the ranger was one of them. Besides, judging from the anger smoldering in those gray eyes of his, ready to explode into flames with the tiniest puff of encouragement, arguing wouldn't have done any good.

Instead she simply nodded.

When he was gone, she set the .45 on the coffee table, pulled her legs onto the couch and curled herself around a throw pillow. Yet tired as she was, she could not rest.

Thoughts of the ranger circled her mind like a captured jaguar pacing the perimeter of his cage.

He could have rejected her when he found out about her connection with the resistance movement. She had expected him to. If not last night, then this morning, after he had a chance to think about it.

He had lain here in the solitary hours before dawn, she realized. Right in this spot where she now lay. She could still smell his faint trace in the pillow—sandalwood and mint toothpaste.

At some point as he stared into the darkness, he must have hated her. She represented everything he loathed. She reminded him that his brother had died for nothing— a collateral casualty in someone else's cause.

She wondered if he still hated her. And if he did, why he was trying so hard to protect her.

Because he had promised?

If so, he was a fool. Promises were an outdated notion. Honor a thing of the past. The world was fluid today. Situations changed. People reciprocated.

Eduardo had promised her a life in America, too, hadn't he? Look what had happened to him.

Elisa burrowed her cheek into the pillow. She didn't want to think of the ranger meeting the same end as Eduardo, but the awful imagery filled her mind anyway. He was out chasing the shadowy man who had been watching them last night. And when a man chased shadows, who knew what danger he would find in the dark?

"Have a beer, Chuckie." After all, Del had already had several. Since he wasn't a drinker, the alcohol hit his bloodstream hard and fast.

Charles Wellesey pushed his wire-rimmed glasses up his hawkish nose and scruffed his kinky red hair. Charles worked in the Department of Public Safety communications office. Del had tried asking questions of his other sources, but nothing had panned out, so he'd called Chuckie. Those comm guys knew everything before it happened, from budget cuts among the office staff to pissing contests among the brass.

"Look, no offense, man," Charles said. "But I don't want to be seen with you."

Del took a hit from his longneck. "Word's already out, huh?"

"Word was out before you left the office."

Bastards. That meant they'd known before he went in what the outcome would be.

Once the six-o'clock news hit the air, the whole world would know. That gave him ten minutes.

"Who was that guy who came in with the director today?" At least Del thought he came in with the director. He wasn't too sure on that point. Just playing a hunch.

"What guy?" Charles picked at the veneer on the bar.

"Ah, ah, ah." Del waggled his beer bottle. "You hold out on me, and I'm gonna have to tell your fiancé about you and that girl from accounting on the copy machine."

"Geez, Cooper." Charles looked over both shoulders to see if anyone was in earshot. "All right, really. What guy?"

"Tall, gray suit, 'big arse' written on his forehead."

"Oh, that guy." Charles leaned close. "Word is he's from Washington."

Del feigned awe. "The apple state?"

"D.C., you moron. How many beers have you had?"

Del declined to answer that. He'd lost count.

"He's a Fed," Charles said, sounding suitably impressed.

"This Fed got a name?"

"Not that I heard."

"What agency?"

"Dunno that, either." He slid off his stool. "I really gotta get out of here. The wrong person sees me talking to you, my career is toast."

Del saluted him with his bottle. "Comm guys don't have careers, Chuckie. They have cubicles."

"Jerk."

"Damn straight."

Before Charles left, he gave Del one last look. "For what it's worth, doesn't seem right, what they did to you."

Del just stared until the man walked away.

"Damn straight," he finally muttered when Charles was gone.

Nine minutes later, the six-o'clock news came on the TV set above the bar. Del motioned for the bartender to turn up the sound as his face appeared under the banner "Fired!"

Wondering if his grandfather was watching the news tonight, Del ordered another beer. This one with a Wild Turkey chaser.

Elisa woke to a faint scratching sound. She jolted in her half sleep, fearing it was rats. Then she realized she was in the ranger's living room, not the filthy basement where she had been taken after she was arrested in San Ynez. There were no piles of garbage or human waste. No rats.

The scraping sound came through the dark again, from the vicinity of the door, then something metal clanked to the floor and the murmur of a guttural curse penetrated the wall.

Moving slowly, silently, Elisa reached for the gun the ranger had left her and pointed the barrel at the darkened entryway. The door lock clacked, and a dark figure barely distinguishable as a man stepped through. He dropped a key ring and didn't bother to pick it up.

Elisa pulled back the slide on the pistol. The moonlight filtering through the window gleamed off the black steel. The silhouette raised his hands like a prisoner. A bright, white smile knifed through the darkness as the silhouette said, "Honey, I'm home."

The gun fell from Elisa's hand and clattered to the table.

"I could have shot you!" she said.

"But you don't believe in violence," he replied.

Shock cut off her mind's ability to reply, then fury brought a course of expletives to her tongue.

Elisa stormed into the bedroom. She stayed there while the ranger bumped down the dark hall. A moment later the light came on in the bathroom, and she heard water running. Finally curiosity got the better of her.

The door was open, so she leaned against the doorjamb and poked her head inside. Every nerve snapped to attention. "You're hurt!"

The ranger held a washcloth to a cut above his left eye and a hand towel to his split lip. Blood mixed with the running water in the sink and ran pink down the drain.

"S'nothing," the ranger said. His words were slurred, more from the effects of the alcohol she could smell on him like cheap perfume than his injuries, she guessed. "You should see the other guy. All four of him."

"One man you were seeing four of, or four different men?"

"Two men I was seeing double of. Get it, two times

two…or is that two plus two?'' He reached to hang the towel back on the bar and stumbled. She caught him.

''Did you drive home like this?''

''Tried to. But the cabbie wouldn't give me his keys,'' he said, chuckling at his own joke.

At least he was a happy drunk. It could be worse. Much, much worse, given what she had heard on television tonight.

Why did he not tell her he had been fired?

She turned his swollen cheek gently. ''Your face,'' she said, her heart twisting at all he'd suffered because of her.

''S'all right. Nothin' could hurt worse than…''

''Than what?''

He drew a heavy breath. ''Than lookin' at you knowing what I did to you. To Eduardo.'' He took a stumbling step to the bedroom.

Stunned, Elisa almost failed to catch him. Just in time she looped one of his arms over her head and ducked under his shoulder. ''Come on, you need to lie down.''

She helped him stumble to the bedroom, flipped on a lamp and pushed him down to the bed. He landed spread-eagle on his back atop the king-size mattress, still grinning. ''You're very pretty when you're disgusted with me.''

''See if you can get your clothes off,'' she said, shaking her head. ''I'll get you an ice pack.''

By the time she returned, he had flipped to his stomach and turned off the lamp. His eyes were closed and his clothes were still on. He had made some attempt to follow instructions, though. One of his boots lay on its side on the floor. The other hung cockeyed off the end of his foot. He looked like a little boy, too worn out from a day's play to do more than throw himself down and sleep.

A very large little boy, with broad shoulders, a long firm body and a tight backside.

Chastising herself for noticing, Elisa turned the lamp on again, sat on the side of the bed and dabbed at one swollen eye with towel and ice. "I thought you were going to get undressed."

"Thought you might want to help," he mumbled, eyes still closed.

She smiled, as much at the girlish flutter in her stomach as at his drunken flirting. "In your dreams."

"Been there, done that."

Elisa's hand went still. Did he really dream about her? Or was his joking just a way to cover the pain?

And avoid the conversation they both knew they needed to have.

After several long seconds of contemplation, she resumed her ice treatment. When she finally found the courage, she asked, "Why didn't you tell me you had been fired?"

"I was…ashamed," he said into the arm pillowing his head.

"You have done nothing to be ashamed of."

His back shuddered. "I didn't see him, Elisa. I looked into that warehouse and I saw a man with a gun. Just one man. Why didn't I see Eduardo?"

"I do not know."

He rolled over. His eyes opened but squinted, heavy lidded, against the glare of the lamp. "Are you sure?"

"What?" She stopped dabbing at his face. Surely she had not heard him right.

"Tell me you didn't know what was going down in there."

''Why?'' The cold from the ice in her hands seeped up Elisa's arms to her heart. ''What do you think I've done?''

With a great deal of effort, he arched his hips off the bed and pulled a folded square of paper from the hip pocket of his jeans. Collapsing back to the mattress, he handed it to her. ''The other man at the warehouse, the one with the gun, was from San Ynez. A member of your *resistance.*'' His lip curled on the final word.

''You think I was buying arms for my cause?'' Temper flared like a sunspot. She almost flung the paper back at him. Despite their differing political views, she had thought he knew her better than this, trusted her more. She started to tell him so, but a long look at his slack, swollen face and the defeat in his gray eyes reminded her of all he had lost today.

He had a right to know what he had lost it *for.*

She took a deep breath, unfolded the tattered sheet and studied the man it pictured. Exhaling slowly, she gave the paper back. ''I do not know this man. And I know nothing of what was happening in the warehouse that day.''

His hand fell limply to the edge of the mattress. The piece of paper fluttered to the thick beige carpet.

Unsure whether that meant he believed her or not, unsure if even he knew, with the alcohol clouding his mind, she rose to leave.

Turning over, he stopped her with a hand on her wrist. ''Don't go.'' His voice was rough, thoroughly male, and sent a purely female response skittering through her veins. She hesitated, torn between the feelings for him that had been growing all week and the residue of her anger. How could he even have thought her capable of brokering weapons?

But then, he wasn't in full control of his faculties tonight. Which made her wonder if it was he who asked her to stay, or the alcohol.

"You need to rest," she said, breaking his grip on her and folding his arm across his chest.

As she started again to leave, he flopped his wrist over his eyes and mumbled, "I told 'im you weren't involved. I told him."

She stopped. "Told who?"

Frowning, he jerked his head to the side. Either he didn't know, or he wasn't willing to name her accuser. "He didn't believe me. Said I had to let you go. Send you back, or else."

She sat on the edge of the bed. Was this true? He had been threatened?

"Told 'im I couldn't do that," he said, his words sharper. She would not have thought he had the strength, but he raised his hand, traced the line of her jaw and tangled his fingers in her hair. The touch, and his voice when he spoke again, was soft. "I would never do that. I promised you."

His promise. Was that all that held him to her? Foolishly she hoped there was more.

His hand still wrapped in her hair, he tugged her toward him, not hurting, just guiding her close. "Don't go," he said again, barely a whisper.

And this time she didn't. She switched off the bedside lamp, took his hand from her hair, clasped it in both of hers. He turned to his side, facing her in the dark, and she stretched out in front of him.

A thick forearm dragged her tightly against him.

His heart lurched unevenly against her back. His breath warmed her shoulder. His breathing gradually became deeper until she thought he slept, but out of the dark, a last soulful murmur reached out to her.

"They're going to press charges against me for shooting Eduardo. Negligent homicide."

Her heart stopped beating. She was afraid to move. Afraid to turn in his arms and offer him the comfort he deserved, lest he stop before he told her all of it.

"They're going to put me in a cage, 'Lis," he slurred, nearly asleep. "Lock me up like an animal."

Elisa's heart nearly tore in two. Now she understood this morning's "errands." He was preparing to leave her, making sure she had everything she needed to live here, alone, while he was gone.

Stubborn fool. He was going to let them send him to prison rather than break his promise to her.

She could not let that happen.

She had already turned the ranger's life upside down. Because of her he had lied to his family and lost his job. She would not let him lose his freedom, too.

She was not sure who was so afraid of her that he would ruin a good man's life to see her sent back to San Ynez, but she had her suspicions.

Tomorrow she would share them.

Chapter 11

Del woke to the sound of gunfire. Three sharp reports— *bam, bam, bam!* The cop part of him screamed to get up, take cover, get the bad guys. The hung-over part pulled a pillow over his head and groaned.

The doorknob rattled. Hinges creaked. Wishing whoever was coming to finish him off would just hurry up and get it over with, he opened one eye.

And saw Elisa slide through the door, a cup of coffee in one hand and two little white pills in the other.

The popping he'd heard hadn't been gunshots after all. Elisa's knocks had just sounded like cannon fire to his throbbing head.

Gliding across the room, she smiled brightly. Damn, she looked good. Even through his bleary eyes. She had on a pair of white shorts that set off her long, tanned legs, and a V-neck top that set off her—

Holy Mother. He'd slept with her. She'd slept with him, rather.

"Good morning," she said, reaching the bed. "Coffee or aspirin first?"

He closed his one open eye and burrowed deeper under the covers. "Neither."

The memories came in fragments. Elisa pressing ice to a face that must have looked like something out of a *Rocky* movie. Elisa holding his hand.

Him asking her to stay.

He was relatively sure he hadn't been in any condition to do anything they'd both regret. But, geez, he hoped he hadn't done anything to embarrass himself, either. Or her.

The covers jerked out of his hands. The brilliance of a full morning sun hit him between the eyes like a wrecking ball.

"What is it they say in Texas?" Elisa the cover ripper asked. "Up and at 'em, cowboy?"

He groaned. "You know what else they say in Texas?"

She quirked an eyebrow.

"He who pokes his fingers in a rattlesnake nest better know how to tie his sneakers with just one hand."

Nonplussed, she set the coffee on the bedside table. Del's nose wrinkled at the scented steam wafting his way. The coffee smelled strong, the way he liked it. His stomach rumbled.

"You have visitors," Elisa said. "Your ranger friends."

Del frowned, and decided against the coffee for the time being. His stomach wasn't ready to go to work yet this morning. "What do they want?"

"To help."

"There's nothing they can do."

"That's not what they say."

He thought about how Mr. Baseball—a Fed, supposedly—had manipulated the director of the DPS, the shooting investigation, even a judge, if the man could produce an arrest warrant as he claimed. Enough lives had been ruined by this thing. ''I don't want to involve them.''

''You didn't. I did.'' Elisa pulled a fresh shirt and pair of jeans from his bureau and handed them to him.

''How's that?''

She opened his bureau again, this time digging through his underwear drawer, shoving aside without comment the box of condoms he kept there. When she turned to answer, she held two white socks and a pair of navy-blue boxers.

Del had had a healthy interest in women since he'd been about fourteen. Over the years he'd found his tastes leaned toward women who wore little black dresses and high heels, hung out in upscale bars and liked to dance. He'd never imagined a scene as domestic as a woman wearing shorts and flat sandals, standing there with his underwear in her arms, could be so appealing.

Then again, they were in his bedroom.

''I called them,'' she said.

He turned his mind off sex and back to the subject at hand. ''Why?''

She hesitated, sat next to him on the bed. ''It was the only way I could think of to help you.''

''I must have really scared you last night if you went to the *policía* for help. I thought you didn't trust cops.''

''I am beginning to trust one, I think.'' She looked at him, and the brush of her gaze against his felt like a caress. Then she grinned and thunked the underwear against his chest. ''Now, get dressed. Your friends are waiting.''

She stood and turned to leave.

"Wait," he called, throwing back the covers and standing so suddenly the motion had him clutching his head. Thankfully she waited patiently while he pushed the nausea back. Even more thankfully, he realized he still had on his jeans from yesterday. "About last night. I just wanted to tell you…"

"There is no need to apologize."

"Yes, there is. But that isn't what I was going to say. I wanted to tell you…thanks. For taking care of me."

What he wanted to do was kiss her, but he wasn't sure she'd appreciate it, despite the warmth shining in her dark-coffee eyes. He didn't feel much like a prince at the moment. Probably didn't look much like one, either.

"You are welcome," she said, then waved her hand toward the bathroom. "Now go. We have much to do."

Del was right—Elisa did not trust the police.

But she was working on it.

He had not let her down, had he?

In fact, he far surpassed her expectations. She had agreed to this pretense of marriage, believing they would never be more than uneasy accomplices. She never thought she would come to depend on his sturdy resolve, to admire his loyalty to family and duty. To desire the crush of his full mouth on hers.

Their relationship had progressed further in their short time together than she could have guessed. They still stood on opposite sides of a political line. But they had learned to work together for a common cause. They had become friends and now, she sensed, teetered on the brink of becoming lovers.

Whether they fell over that edge or not might well depend on what happened today. There was much to discuss. Some of it would be difficult, especially in front of others. But it was time to tell her husband the whole truth, no matter how difficult.

And hope that he would understand.

She topped off the rangers' coffee cups while he showered. Kat Solomon drank hers—when she stopped talking long enough to drink—with so much cream and sugar she might as well have had a milk shake. Clint Hayes added a little water to temper the heat, and Captain Matheson took his coffee straight up, the way he took his conversation.

"I hate to say it. But with a liberal jury and a lot of spin, a good prosecutor might get a conviction on negligence. What will you do if Del goes to jail, ma'am?" he asked.

Liberate him, she wanted to say. The way she had liberated many of her people held unjustly in San Ynez. She recognized the idea as a foolish thought, though. This was not San Ynez, where prisoners were housed in old school gymnasiums and guarded by drunks. And these were Texas Rangers she was talking to. She did not think they would appreciate her fervor for undermining the American penitentiary system.

"I would prefer to see that doesn't happen," she answered instead.

"Don't you worry," Kat piped in. "We've already done some legwork. Got the name of this bar where Garcia used to hang out a lot and—"

"Kat!" The captain stood her down with a stare. "Let's wait for Del, why don't we?"

Elisa estimated that meant they would take the cue from their friend on whether or not to share their information with her.

"Don't worry, Kat," Elisa heard her ranger call from behind her. "Won't be a long wait."

There was an empty seat between the female ranger and Clint, but Del dragged a decorative chair from against the wall and wedged himself in next to Elisa. His hair was wet and his shirt clung to his damp skin, testifying to his superior body. One eye was bruised and puffy, but his smile had returned.

"Holy moly, Cooper," Kat said. "Your face looks like one of my nephew Austin's crayon drawings. His favorite color is purple."

"You get it all out of your system?" the captain asked. Nobody had to clarify what Del had needed to purge. Anger was one of those universal truths everyone understood.

"For now," Del said.

"Good enough." The captain scanned the faces around the table. "Let's get to work."

"Before we start," Del offered, "there's something I want to say."

He paused to clear his throat, his friends waiting expectantly.

"I just...I mean...I'm sorry about the way I acted yesterday. I was mad, but I shouldn't have taken it out on all of you."

Silence surrounded the table a moment, then Clint drolled, "Ouch. That must'a hurt," and the tension snapped like a dry twig.

"Clint," Kat warned, elbowing him, then smiled across the table. "That's really sweet, Del. We knew you didn't mean anything by it. Heck, if you can't lean on your friends when times get tough—"

The captain scooted his chair back, scraping the legs on the tile floor. "Apology accepted. Now can we get on with this? Mrs., ah, Cooper, you said you had something to tell us?''

''Call me Elisa, please.''

Del looked at her curiously while she prepared herself with a deep breath. Her nerves buzzed, both afraid of his reaction to the truth she was about to tell and relieved to finally have it out.

''Del told me,'' she said, looking at the ranger captain, ''that he could not be held accountable for Eduardo's death if Eduardo was part of the transaction taking place in the warehouse.''

Captain Matheson nodded. ''If he went there to conduct criminal activity, then he knowingly put himself at risk. The liability is his, not Del's. But we have no proof that Garcia was involved in the arms deal. Are you telling us you do?''

''Not proof, perhaps, as your courts demand. But suspicions.''

Del's eyes turned cold as chips of ice. ''You said the resistance doesn't buy guns.''

Though her stomach twisted at the implied accusation, she didn't blame him for his suspicion. She had never been totally honest with him—until today.

''The resistance does not,'' she said. Looking around the table, she wondered if any of the rangers, with their Uncle Sam and their red-white-and-blue upbringing, could believe the depravity of the leadership that controlled her country. ''But the military might.''

Even stone-faced Clint showed his surprise. ''You're saying someone in the U.S. is selling guns to a foreign government? That's a majorly serious offense.''

Del studied her curiously. ''And knowing who the guns were for doesn't help me any.''

''Unless it was Eduardo doing the buying,'' she said quietly.

The captain frowned. ''What makes you think Garcia was connected to the San Ynez army?''

''When I met him, he was injured in an army attack. His wound infected. In his fever, he talked of El Presidente finally taking his rightful place as leader of San Ynez.'' Bile boiled in Elisa's throat as she thought of Sanchez, the butcher, and his illegally gained power in her country. There was nothing rightful about assassination. ''I thought his rambling no more than the delusions of illness, but later, after he recovered, he began to ask questions. About the resistance. Especially about our leader. I began to wonder if his presence in that village, on that day—even his injuries—had really been an accident. Colonel Sanchez has sent spies before to infiltrate the resistance before. To learn the identity of La Puma, our leader. What better way to earn our trust than to be wounded supporting the cause?''

''So you sent him away.'' Kat looked as entranced as a teenage girl at a romantic movie. Only this wasn't any movie. This was Elisa's life. ''Even though you…cared for him.''

Elisa nodded. ''Yes.'' It had been a hurtful time for her. A time when the mantle of responsibility threatened to crush her beneath its weight.

''Because you couldn't risk exposing your people's leader?''

Her mouth turned dry as powder as she gathered herself to tell the rest. She could not bear to look at Del for fear of the recrimination she might see.

She swallowed painfully. Del had accepted some of who—and what—she was. Feelings had developed between them despite their different backgrounds. If those feelings were to grow, he had to know the whole truth about her. If he couldn't accept it, then their relationship was as flimsy as their marriage.

She raised her chin. Carefully met his measured gaze. "Because I *am* my people's leader."

Del leaned against the jamb at the bedroom door, watching as Elisa brushed her hair. Despite the questions he needed to ask, now that the other rangers were gone and he could voice them in private, he paused to watch. The image of her in the mirror, stroking a brush repeatedly through the silky black waterfall of her hair, seemed so feminine, so serene. Totally at odds with his idea of a woman who was not only involved with a third-world insurgent party, but had founded it.

She'd never intended to become the guiding force behind the resistance in her country, she'd said. But when, after spending three days imprisoned in the dark without food or water, she'd escaped, she'd lead her brothers and three other prisoners to freedom with her. From that point forward, they looked to her for direction. Together they'd vowed not to rest until all those whom Colonel Sanchez held unjustly were free.

She hadn't wanted the responsibility of being their leader. Circumstance had called her to the role.

Which made Del wonder how she had found it so easy to walk away—especially to go to a man she considered a traitor to his people.

"You knew," he said as she raked the brush down the length of her hair again, "that Garcia wasn't just some bleeding-heart world-aid worker."

"I suspected," she corrected.

Their eyes met in the mirror.

"You were going to marry him, anyway."

"I had a baby to think about."

"All this about saving your people from tyranny, fighting for freedom, is just rhetoric, then. Easily abandoned when it's inconvenient."

"No."

"He was your *enemy*."

"He was the father of my child."

Del felt a pang of regret when she set the hairbrush down and turned. He could happily pass a whole day watching her brush her hair.

Annoyed with himself for admitting it, even to himself, he shoved his shoulder off the door frame and stood straight. What he needed now was to focus on the conversation at hand, not personal hygiene.

But as she stepped toward him, sunlight streamed in the window beside them, gilding her almond complexion in a healthy glow. Her sleek body was ripening with pregnancy, he realized. Both her abdomen and her breasts were fuller, heavier.

A longing to touch those breasts, to measure their new weight in his palms, test their sensitivity with his thumbs, struck him like a blow. The impact sang along the nerves in his arms to make his fingers tingle and ran down his spine to settle as an ache between his legs.

Damn, he'd been so close last night. He'd had her in his arms. If he hadn't been so drunk...

She stopped in front of him. The familiar scent of vanilla and almond surrounded him. Del inhaled deeply.

Then jolted himself out of his lecherous fantasy before he did something stupid, like pulled her against him and let her feel the reaction she stirred in him.

"I am not proud of all I've done. But I had no proof that Eduardo was not what he claimed, no evidence other than the ramblings of delirium. And I was being hunted in San Ynez,'' she said, her coffee eyes serious. ''Sanchez's captains promised him they would crush the resistance—starting with its leader. The soldiers were everywhere. It was difficult to escape them at times before I was pregnant. Carrying a baby, I could not have survived. My *child* could not have survived.''

Del tried to concentrate on her words, and not the tomtom beat of blood in his groin. ''So you just left. Left your people to fend for themselves in the middle of the hornet's nest you stirred up.''

''No. I have twin brothers, Miguel and Raul. They were only sixteen when the resistance began. Too young for the responsibilities of leadership. But they have grown. They are twenty-four now, and seasoned. They have been—how do you say in Texas?—'chomping at the bit' to take control for a long time. Now El Puma can be in two places at once. They will not let my people down.''

She raised her hand toward him, as if she could make him feel the truth in her words, if only she could touch him. Her fingers hovered inches from his bruised cheek.

His breath caught. His heart stuttered. He pulled his head back. He didn't want her fingers on his face. He wanted to draw them into his mouth and suckle each perfect pink fingertip.

He restrained himself from following through on that desire. Barely.

A sweat broke between his shoulder blades. This was crazy. She represented everything he loathed. People turning against their own flag. Civil unrest.

Vulnerable women, widowed by war, left to raise their babies alone, as his mother had been.

Del blinked back a wave of emotion. Vulnerable, hell. Elisa might have some uncertainties about her pregnancy and her future in the U.S., but she was the strongest woman he knew. He'd always seen the noble pride in her. The determination. Now when he looked at her, he saw the courage, too. He couldn't imagine the kind of heart it took for a twenty-year-old girl to escape from prison, organize her people and stand up against an entire government.

He didn't want to imagine it. Because imagining Elisa with that kind of courage meant admitting that everything he had done had been for nothing. Getting married, loosing his job—none of it mattered. A woman who could lead an entire freedom movement would have found a way to protect her baby, with or without his help.

Maybe she hadn't come to the U.S. for the baby's sake at all.

Del used the heat from his unwanted lust to fuel his anger. "Tell me. What would you have done if you'd married Garcia and then found out he was supplying Sanchez with guns?"

Her confidence wavered, along with her voice. "I do not know."

"You must have thought about it."

"I...I hoped I would find it was not true."

"Would you have killed him?"

Elisa's eyes opened wide. She stepped back. Knowing he was being irrational, that he'd gone too far, didn't stop Del. This whole thing had gone too far. The investigation. The threats...

He stepped forward, closing the gap she'd opened between them, allowing her no room. No escape, this time.

"Was that your mission all along?"

"My *mission?*"

"Is that why you slept with him in the first place? To get him to talk? Find out if he was working for Sanchez?'' He raked a hand across his forehead. ''Hell of a strategy. Screw him. Have his baby. Kill him. Anything for the cause, right?''

She wanted to slap him. He could see it in her eyes. To her credit she squeezed her hand into a fist at her side instead. ''How lucky for me, then, that you came along,'' she said as quietly as a serpent's sibilant warning. ''I did not have to murder him. You did it for me.''

If she'd swung a baseball bat between his legs, she couldn't have taken the breath from him faster. Or more completely.

She tried to slide past him, out of the bedroom. Recovering just in time, he reached back, slapped his palm flat against the door panel and slammed it shut. His arm blocked her passage.

''I did what I had to and you damn well know it,'' he gritted out.

She surprised him by nodding. ''You were protecting your friend. I have accepted that. It is you who cannot accept that I also have done what I had to do, to protect my people and my child.''

Just like that, her quiet righteousness robbed him of his fury. She was right. Who was he to judge her?

A fool, that's who. He'd tried to contain his anger at himself over the mistake he'd made at the warehouse, but it kept spilling out. Mostly onto her. She'd borne the brunt of his frustration since the day he'd found her at the cemetery chapel, and put up with it virtually without complaint. Even pretended their relationship might be growing beyond a mere marriage of necessity.

She'd let him kiss her. Hold her.

Because she needed him to keep her baby safe.

She'd done what she had to do.

Was that really all there was between them? Damn it,

why did it matter so much to him? He wasn't supposed to care about her. She was a duty to him, nothing more. A way to right a wrong, clear his conscience.

At least, he'd thought that's all she was.

His stomach turned sickly. With his right hand still flat against the door, he swung his body around hers, planting his left palm on the door, too, and trapping her between his arms. "If I said I accepted all of it—you being La Puma, the resistance, Garcia—what then?"

He leaned so close to her that he could feel his breath reflected from her face, but she didn't budge. She didn't push him away, didn't tell him to go to hell. No, she kept too much inside to show that kind of emotion, just like he did.

Instead she dabbed her lips with the tip of her tongue, and sent his body temperature soaring.

"It would be a start, I guess," she said.

A start to what? Two years of anorexic marriage leading up to a divorce on the day she met her permanent residency requirements? Friendship? Pop-your-eyeballs-out, total-body-workout sex?

He had no doubt sex would be great between them. When two people who kept so much bottled up inside themselves finally let go, the results were bound to be explosive.

Maybe that's exactly what both of them needed. A little release.

A lot of releases.

Now that he knew she not only hadn't been in love with Garcia, but had suspected him, however faintly of being a traitor to her people, there was no reason to hold back. She wouldn't be betraying Garcia, and Del didn't have to feel guilty about taking another man's woman.

There was a great big bed behind him, and he had time to kill.

He lowered his head until their noses bumped, nudged to find the right fit. He angled his head and shared her next breath, taking it deep inside himself. He gazed into her rich, dark eyes.

And then he stopped.

He couldn't do this now. Not when this storm of desire he was caught in had been whipped into existence by anger. And not with her looking at him like a yearling heifer cornered by a full-grown Brahma bull.

He hadn't exactly given her a chance to catch up to him, going from accusing her of plotting murder to wanting to commit acts with her that might still be illegal in several states in about six and a half seconds.

Besides, he didn't want to mate with her in a frenzy of pent-up frustration channeled into lust. He wanted to take his time with her. Savor her. He wanted her to be as desperate for him as he was for her.

He leaned his forehead against hers. On the door his hands curled into fists, but he didn't pull them away. If he did, he might touch her. And if he touched her, he wouldn't stop until he'd touched every inch of her.

"I guess a start is better than an end," he said, his mouth against her temple. He couldn't resist lowering his head to nibble at her cheek with his lips. "Especially since we haven't even gotten to the good part yet."

"The good part?" For someone who had been standing still the past five minutes, she sounded remarkably out of breath.

He smiled into her hair, liking the effect he had on her. "The part where I tell you what an amazing, courageous, indomitable-spirited woman I think you are."

"Mmm." She tipped her head back to give him access

to her throat. Against his better judgment, he coursed his mouth over the creamy column.

"And you tell me what a strong, hot hunk of man I am, and how much you want me."

"Ah," she said.

He raised his head in time to see her eyes open, focus. He hadn't felt her move, but her hands were fisted in his shirt.

"That would be the part where you're dreaming," she said, and gave him a little shove back as she ducked under his arm to freedom.

He probably should have taken offense, or at least felt mildly rejected, but before he could round up enough brain cells to think about anything other than the clean taste of her and the intoxicating scent of her skin, he caught her grinning. She tried to press her lips back into a straight line, failed and let a laugh burst through her smile.

He shifted position, propping one shoulder against the door and trying to look casual despite evidence to the contrary pushing at the fly of his jeans. "Dreaming, huh?"

She shrugged, half apologetic, half wickedly encouraging. The little flirt. She was teasing him.

Torturing him, actually.

He narrowed his eyes at her seriously. Turnabout was fair play. "That's all right. Go ahead and laugh. Guess your mother never told you."

"Told me what?"

"If you work hard enough for what you want, dreams do come true." Her smile sobered while his grew. "And I've always been a very hard worker."

Very hard.

Chapter 12

Elisa clutched the door handle as Del swung into the parking space next to Captain Matheson's forest-green pickup. It was only one o'clock in the afternoon, but already a half dozen cars, along with at least as many Harley-Davidson motorcycles, littered the lot outside The Last Buck Saloon, their owners presumably inside. Above the door, a neon cowboy tipped his hat with each kick of his mount's hind legs and bold green letters flashed *Open.*

"You are sure Eduardo came here?" she asked, climbing out of the Rover doubtfully. Broken glass crunched beneath the sole of her shoe. A woman with sunken eyes studied them from the street corner, tugging her pink tube top up and her silver miniskirt down. Despite Elisa's suspicions about Eduardo, she could not picture him choosing this place to spend his free time.

"According to one of the other security guards at the warehouse," Del said. "He and Eduardo stopped by for some beers after work, and the people here seemed to know Eduardo.''

The other rangers had already started for the bar. Del hung back. ''You don't have to go inside.''

''I wish I did not.'' She wished she did not have to face the truth about the man she had planned to marry, the father of her child, but she was part of what was happening to Del now. She belonged at his side. ''But I knew Eduardo. You did not. I might be able to make sense of something he said, or did, when you could not.''

He gave her a second to change her mind, then nodded and guided her toward the door with his hand resting casually in the small of her back. It was a comfortable, reassuring gesture. Nothing remotely sexual about it. And yet Elisa's spine tingled beneath his fingertips as they walked into the seedy bar full of men who had little left to lose. His touch felt thoroughly male, primitively possessive, a silent warning to the beer-bellied bikers tucked into a booth in the corner and the wiry winos at the bar that she belonged to him.

Del nudged Elisa toward the table Kat and Clint had taken in the middle of the room. The captain was already at the bar, showing a picture of Eduardo to a bearded man who was wiping shot glasses down with a stained towel.

''You know this man?'' Matheson asked.

''No.'' The bartender never looked up from his drying.

''Maybe you want to try that again,'' the captain said, leaning close to the bartender. ''This time actually look at the picture before you answer.''

''Don't gotta look. I make it a point not to know no one here. No faces. No names. *Nada.* Especially when it's a cop doing the asking.''

Del held Elisa's chair until she sat, then joined the captain at the bar. "Well, would you look at that? A psychic bartender. He knew you were a Texas Ranger before you even showed him your badge, Bull."

"Texas Ranger?" The man set down the last shot glass and ambled a few feet down the bar. Del followed. "Don't care if you're freaking Canadian Mounties. I don't talk to cops."

He slung his towel down on the bar and began wiping. Quick as a snake, Del grabbed it, whipped it around the man's neck and used it to pull him down. "Then you won't have any problem talking to me. I'm not a cop. Not anymore."

The bartender tried to rear back. Del held him down.

The bikers in back got to their feet. Clint reached beneath his jacket, pulled out a shiny pistol and laid it on the table, all without turning to look at the approaching gang. "Take a powder, boys. We don't have any beef with you. Yet."

The bikers shuffled back to their booth.

The bartender rolled his bulging gaze up to Matheson. "You crazy? You're cops. You can't let him do this!"

Matheson looked over to the table. "You hear somebody say something, Hayes?"

"Nah. Nobody in here talks to cops."

"Yeah, that's what I thought." The captain leaned across the bar, filled a glass with tap water and carried it to the table, leaving the photograph behind.

Del wound his towel noose in one fist and reached for the picture. He had such a ferocious look on his face that Elisa might have thought she had been right about *policía* after all—they were all bad—if she hadn't seen him let a half an inch of cloth slide through his hand when the bartender gasped. Del had no intention of hurting anyone. Elisa just hoped the bartender did not know that.

He held Eduardo's picture in front of the barkeep's eyes. "Try again. You know this man?"

"Geez! You're the crazy cop who shot him, aren't you?"

Del tightened his grip. "You figure it out." Del tightened his grip. "Might want to be quick about it, though. Before you run out of air."

The bearded man swore. "So he came in here to drown his troubles. So what?"

Elisa shifted nervously in her seat. Now they were getting somewhere.

A woman wearing a white half apron with a frayed hem and carrying a round serving tray stepped out of the kitchen into the barroom. She was short, maybe five foot four and rail thin. Bleached blond hair spilled out of the clip that held a brittle ponytail off the back of her neck. She walked by Del without a second look, as if men strangled the bartender in here every day.

"Get you some drinks?" Her pen poised over a blank pad, she looked down at the table through eyes as worn as a set of bald tires.

"I'd like a cherry cola," Kat chirped.

At the bar Del narrowed his eyes at his unwilling informant. "Who did Garcia come in with?"

"Nobody. He sat alone, most nights."

"What about when he didn't? You got names?" Del gave the towel a little yank.

The barkeep snarled. "No. You got more pictures?"

"Nothing for me," Clint told the waitress, watching the show with amusement. Her gaze caught on the pistol sitting in plain view. He just smiled at her.

Bull Matheson tipped his water glass at her. "I'm fine, thanks."

"He say anything?" Del asked the bartender. "Talk about his work? Women? Politics? Religion?"

"No, man. He was real quiet. Now get the hell off me!"

"Give me reason."

A string of curses sizzled in the air. "He used the phone sometimes, man. The pay phone in the hall. That's all I know."

Del let go of the towel so suddenly the man's head almost hit the bar. He started toward the table. The bartender glared at his back a moment, then went back to work wiping down the bar. Or at least spreading the filth more evenly.

Del pulled a chair next to the captain. "What do you think our chances are of getting the records on that phone?"

Matheson frowned. A lock of black hair fell over his forehead. "I can try. It'll take a warrant."

Clint holstered his weapon and leaned forward. "Gene might be able to help. Surely there's a judge or two that owes him a favor. And he sure owes you one."

Del rubbed his left thigh. "That was a long time ago."

"Man doesn't forget when someone saves his life."

"It's the only lead we've got," Kat said.

Del took a deep, considering breath. "All right. Ask him."

The waitress brought out Kat's cherry cola and then walked to the bar. As she passed, she stopped to look at the picture of Eduardo Del had left there. Was it Elisa's imagination, or did the woman's shoulders tighten?

A moment later she tossed the picture down with her

serving tray and hurried down the hall toward the bathroom.

Leaving the rangers to their strategizing, Elisa followed.

She found the woman bent over a sink, splashing water on her face. "Are you okay?"

The waitress started as if she had not heard Elisa come in. "I...I'm fine."

"Did you recognize the man in that picture?"

Subtle tension gathered again in the woman's body. "Lalo? Sure. He is—was—a regular here."

Elisa frowned, not sure how to proceed. Interrogation was not a skill she had practiced. She was not sure if the woman lied or was sincere. But something bothered her....

"Did you know him well?" she tried.

The woman shrugged, grabbed a paper towel and patted her face dry. "I served him drinks and sympathy, just like every other guy in here."

"Sympathy for what?"

"Look, I gotta get back to work." She threw her rumpled towel in an overflowing can.

Elisa opened her mouth to ask another question, but the bathroom door popped open. Kat came in, and the waitress left.

"Elisa, are you okay?" Kat asked. "Del was worried about you. He thought you might be...you know... sick."

Still thinking about the waitress, she said, "I am not sick."

"Well, that's good. I told him you were probably fine, but he insisted I come in here and check." Kat squeezed her shoulders up toward her ears. "It was kind of cute, actually. Seeing the tough guy all worried about you."

To Elisa, thoughts of Del and ''cute'' were incongruous. He could be primitively male, intense, dangerous, even seductive. But not cute.

''Look, I never got to tell you how neat I think it is that the two of you—''

Suddenly Elisa was tired of the lies. The pretense. ''You know he only married me because he thought it was his duty.''

''Duty-schmooty,'' Kat said. ''I think it's all about ego. Men just can't stand to admit they might be slightly less than perfect.''

''You sound as if you speak from experience.''

''Boy, how.''

Elisa wasn't sure exactly what that meant, but she took it as a yes. ''So who is this not-so-perfect man in your life?''

Her gaze on the floor, Kat toed the tile. ''Let's just say he's someone whose sense of duty would be much happier if I was a sheep herder in Nova Scotia instead of a Texas Ranger.''

Interesting. But before she could ask another question to narrow down the possibilities for Kat's love interest, a knock sounded on the bathroom door.

Del poked his head in. With a look, he sent Kat on her way. ''You okay?'' he asked when they were alone.

She nodded.

''Good. Then let's roll. We've got all we're going to get here.''

''Maybe we'll get lucky, and the pay phone records will show Eduardo rang right through to Sanchez's private number.''

It was the first thing she'd said in fifteen miles. Del took his eyes off the road long enough to look at her, and cursed himself. She was pale. She hadn't eaten all day. She probably needed a nap.

And yet she was making jokes for his benefit. Only, there was nothing funny about this situation, and they both knew it.

"And maybe Santa Claus will bring me a new life for Christmas this year." He hated that he sounded so pathetic.

She rested her head on the back of the seat. "Make it two. One for each of us."

"Only if I still get to know you," he said softly.

She rolled her head toward him. "Not everything about this life is so bad."

"No. Not everything."

"If you can find Eduardo's accomplices, will it be enough?"

"If Eduardo was involved." It galled him to know that the evidence that might clear him would also prove Elisa had been betrayed by someone she cared about. The father of her child. "It might. But there are no guarantees."

They'd made a good run at clearing his name, but what chance did a handful of rangers and one Amazon princess really have at cracking an international arms conspiracy in less than twenty-four hours?

Knowing he might not have much time with her created a poignant ache in him. He studied her, trying to memorize the elegant shape of her nose, the proud angles of her cheeks. The twenty-four hours Mr. Baseball had given him were almost gone. If Del was going to jail tomorrow, his last night of freedom ought to be one worth remembering.

She caught him watching her. "Is something wrong?"

"No, nothing. You're perfect." He knew how he

wanted to spend the evening. The question was, did she want the same thing?

She smiled self-consciously. "Where are we going?"

"Depends. You feeling tired, or are you up for a little fun and entertainment?"

"I am fine. The fatigue is not so bad as it used to be."

On impulse, he turned south on MacArthur Boulevard. "Then I think it's high time I introduced you to an old Texas tradition. Barbecue."

The Spit-n-Hole looked like a condemned barn on the outside. The inside was even worse. Dusty portraits of famous breeding horses decorated the plank walls. Patrons sat on rough-hewn benches tucked up under the sheets of plywood spanning sawhorses that served as tables. No two plates matched, half the silverware was plastic and the sauce was served in recycled ketchup bottles, but the barbecue was the best in the state. Even on a week night they waited twenty minutes for a table.

"Are you sure about this place?" Elisa asked dubiously as she took her seat in a wobbly chair.

"Positive."

A waitress in a red-and-white-checked blouse, white shorts and white cowboy boots, appeared beside them, menus in hand. Before Elisa could take one, Del said, "We'll have the large meat-eater's platter, corn on the cob and baked beans. A root beer for me, and milk for the lady."

The waitress scuffed away, and Elisa raised an eyebrow at his presumptuousness. "Eat here often?"

"Every chance I get. You mind?"

"I'll let you know after I taste it."

Del didn't sweat that. One bite, and he figured the Spit-n-Hole would have another convert.

He was right. Bliss on her face and barbecue sauce on

all ten fingers, Elisa ate half the sliced beef and more than her share of the pork ribs.

As they gorged themselves, they talked about her twin brothers, Miguel and Raul, and his brother, Sam, though that topic was too sad to linger on for long. Del told her about riding horses on his grandparents' farm as a kid. Elisa regaled him with the story of the time she'd tried to ride a pack burro. With every anecdote, she enchanted him more. By the end of the evening, he couldn't take his eyes off her.

"That was wonderful," she said, wiping the last of the sauce from her lips with a rumpled napkin. "But I don't think it was listed in my prenatal nutrition plan."

"Call it part of her cultural education, then. That kid of ours is going to be a proper Texan, we gotta start her early."

Elisa's hands went still. "Ours?"

"I...I mean yours," he said, backpedaling. Damn, what had he been thinking? One slip of the tongue and he'd put a damper on the whole evening. "I'm sorry."

"No." She smiled at him, and the light from it went straight to the dark recesses of his heart. She reached across the table, her fingertips just brushing his. "I like the sound of 'ours.'"

"Yeah?"

"Yeah."

His heart thumped ridiculously hard. Was it his imagination, or had she just acknowledged him as more than a make-believe husband? If he was misreading her, he was going to make a gigantic fool of himself, but the invitation in her coffee eyes was hard to mistake.

"Well then, seein's how this is culture night, how about we give a whirl to another cornerstone of Texas living? It's called the two-step." Linking his fingers with hers, he pulled her up from the table and toward the fifteen-by-fifteen bare patch of hardwood in the corner that passed as a dance floor at the Spit-n-Hole. On the way there, he sunk three quarters in the jukebox.

When the first song came on, a George Strait ballad, he lifted their linked hands to the side, rested his other hand on her hip and gave her a quick lesson in the one, two and three shuffle that formed the basis of country and western dancing.

She stared down at her feet as he set off in slow motion, counting for her. "You're going to make me try this in front of all these people?"

"Nobody's watching," he lied. Every male in the place was staring at her. Elisa was the kind of woman who naturally drew attention. She seemed to be the only one who didn't know it.

She made it through the first whirling turn, and Del felt her relax into the motion. She was a quick learner. "Why do they call this the two-step when there are three steps?" she asked as he counted off another set for her.

"I don't know."

"It should be the three-step," she insisted.

He laughed at her seriousness. "That's a different dance."

"How many steps does it have?"

"I don't know. Four probably."

"Humph," she said, taking the next turned with a little extra flair that said she'd definitely found the rhythm. "Texans."

By the end of the tune, Elisa danced as if she'd been two-stepping all her life. Which was a good thing, since the second song he'd punched up on the jukebox was a bit faster. A lot faster, actually. Del added a twirl to their routine that had her spinning out to the end of his grip, then reeling back in so fast that her hair flared around her as she twisted, tangling them both, tying them together.

They were both in need of a little oxygen when the song ended.

"Was that a dance?" Elisa asked between gusty breaths. "Or a training exercise?"

He struggled to regulate his own erratic breathing. "What's wrong? Can't keep up?"

"I'm dancing for two."

"In that case, I think you'll like the next song."

Garth Brooks crooned from the speakers. Elisa cocked her head and listened to the first few strains. "If tomorrow never comes?"

"Seemed fitting," he said, suddenly wishing he'd picked something different. He hoped she didn't read too much into his choice of music. Or maybe he hoped she did.

Whichever the case, he wasn't complaining about the results. Elisa leaned into him, rested her cheek on his shoulder. He tightened his hold on her, bringing their bodies into the kind of steady contact he'd craved all night.

Awe lit up his nerves at the feel of her heart kicking against his ribs. Her pulse bounding off his fingertips as he changed his grip and curled their linked hands inward to cradle against his shoulder. Awe changed to reverence as the friction between them built, and her breasts flattened against his chest, her hips caressed his.

She looked up at him and smiled her approval. This close, there were no secrets between them. When the last refrain faded to silence, they gazed deep into each other's eyes, still body to body.

"Do you want me to put some more money in the

jukebox?'' he asked, surprised he was still able to form a coherent thought with her this close.

"No."

He swallowed hard. "Do you want some dessert?"

"No."

"Then what do you want?"

She disengaged her hand from his and traced his swollen bottom lip with her thumb. There was no mistaking her meaning, but just to be sure, she added, "I want you to take me home."

Del couldn't pay the bill fast enough. Then he dropped his keys in the parking lot. If he didn't cool off, they were going to wind up in a ditch off I-35 tonight instead of in his big bed.

By some miracle they were still in one piece when they turned onto his block. But as he cruised up to the Randolph gate, he knew the night wasn't going to turn out as he'd hoped.

A Dallas PD black-and-white sitting dark on the street came to life as he passed and pulled in behind him at the big iron gate.

"Damn it!" He pounded the steering wheel with his fist.

Elisa looked out the rear window worriedly. Two uniformed officers were working their way carefully toward the Land Rover, right hands resting on their gun holsters. "What is it? What do they want?"

"It's all right. Just sit quiet and do what they tell you."

The officer on the driver's side tapped on the glass. Del lowered the window and shut off the engine.

"Delgado Cooper?" the officer asked.

"Yes."

"Step out of the vehicle please, sir. I have a warrant for your arrest."

Chapter 13

"Damn."

Clint Hayes's curse reeled Del toward reality from the black depths of the memories of last night playing on a continuous loop in his mind. He'd arrested a lot of men, seen them processed through the legal system.

He never thought he'd be one of them.

"Fingertips on the glass one at a time. Roll them left to right." "Strip." "Open your mouth." "Spread your legs."

He'd done what he was told without speaking, without looking at any of them. The more he cooperated, the sooner it would be over, or so he'd hoped.

The nightmare trip from the sally port, where prisoners were admitted, to his jail cell had taken three humiliating hours. Worse, by the time he'd been processed it was too late to go before a magistrate, which meant it had been morning before he could bail himself out of that hell hole.

He'd spent the night stretched out on a narrow, stainless steel bunk that resembled a slab in the morgue more than any bed. Sleep eluded him, so he passed the hours mentally replaying every excruciating second of his booking over and over until the jailhouse lights had finally gone from dim to bright and the bailiff had come to lead him down the long hall to the judge's bench.

When he'd left the courtroom, freed on his own recognizance—the only luxury he'd been afforded for his fourteen years of service to the state of Texas—Kat had been waiting in the hall. She waved him to a side entrance, where Clint sat waiting in a rumbling Dodge Ram truck, strategically out of view of the TV news vans and newspaper reporters crowding the court steps.

"Elisa?" Del asked, though he was already sure she was the one who had called his friends. For a woman who didn't like cops, she was getting pretty cozy with his teammates—former teammates.

Hayes nodded.

"She called right after they picked you up," Kat said.

"Not doing your career any good to be helping me."

"Shut up and get in," Hayes said.

Del didn't argue. He would have liked to have told his friends they'd done too much already, insisted on finding his own ride home, but the truth was he wanted to get out of there more than he wanted to be noble and selfless.

Minutes later the deep-throated diesel pickup had left the jail behind, but the stink of incarceration followed Del like ugly on an armadillo.

So did the reporters.

"We were hoping they wouldn't connect you to Randolph just yet," Clint said, glaring at the KDAL news van blocking the drive to Gene's estate. He honked and a flock of microphone-toting, gossipmongering men and women with perfect hair and smiles that loved a camera clustered around the truck, tapping on windows and shouting questions through the glass.

"Mr. Cooper, is it true that Former Governor Gene Randolph posted your bail?"

"How does it feel to be on the inside of the same bars you put so many men behind?"

Del slunk down in his seat. "Like vultures on a carcass," he mumbled.

"More like bottom feeders," Clint said. "Hold on." He rolled the truck forward slowly, honking again. When the van whose tail blocked the entrance to the driveway still didn't move, he gave its bumper a little kiss with the cow catcher on the front of his truck. When it still didn't move, he kissed a little harder.

Finally the van lurched forward. Bull swung the truck into the drive and lowered the window to punch the security code into the panel at the gate.

"Did you kill Eduardo Garcia because you wanted his fiancé for yourself?" a reporter shouted, plunging her microphone through the open window.

"No comment." So they knew about Elisa, too. Great. Just what she needed—to become the center ring of a three-ring media circus. He should never have gotten involved with her. She'd have been better off without his "help."

He couldn't regret marrying her, though. Not just because he was a stubborn jackass who refused to be pushed around by some nameless government power-broker hiding behind federal anonymity, but because she was the only thing that made his miserable life bearable these days.

Because he didn't want to lose her.

God, when had his whole life started to revolve around her?

The second he'd seen her, a little voice in the back of his head said.

He pinched the bridge of his nose and turned his face from the camera shoved against the passenger-side window. The wrought iron gate swung open, and the reporters surged forward.

"Step one foot onto this property," Kat warned them out the rear window, "and I'll have you all hauled off for criminal trespass."

Without waiting for a reaction, Clint put the truck in gear and drove through the entrance. The press stayed behind the gate, but they didn't look happy about it.

The crowd assembled in Del's carriage house apartment didn't look too happy, either. Bull Matheson brooded over a steaming mug at the kitchen table. Across from him, Gene Randolph looked up from his own coffee to peer at Del.

Del cursed himself silently. Gene had been his mentor and his friend. Del hated that he'd returned the favor by bringing trouble to his doorstep.

"Sorry about the mess out front, Gene."

Gene waved his hand in irritation. "Thirty years in politics, and you think I can't handle a few reporters outside my gate? Come sit down and get some food in your belly. You look lower'n a hog in a mud hole."

"I'm not hungry." Del headed for the bedroom. He appreciated his friend's sentiment, but he couldn't stomach either food or company at the moment. All he wanted was a shower.

"I made biscuits." Elisa's quiet voice stopped him halfway across the room. She stood in the kitchen doorway holding a carafe of coffee with a dish towel around the handle. He could see by the circles under her eyes and the tendrils escaping from the French braid she'd woven her hair in that she hadn't slept much more than he had, yet she dredged up a fleeting smile for him. The pure hope in the quick flash of teeth and curl of lush lips sent a spear of longing straight to his gut.

He tore his gaze away and glanced down at the table, where peach, apple and blackberry jelly jars surround a half-eaten plate of sourdough biscuits. No way could he eat with his stomach bubbling like the La Brea Tar Pits, but he didn't want her to think her efforts weren't appreciated.

"This is the second day in a row you've had to cook breakfast for these animals." He found a degree of warmth deep inside him and tried to focus it on her, to let her know with a look that he was okay. At least he would be once he'd had that shower and maybe a little sleep. "Pretty domestic for a guerrilla leader."

She arched one eyebrow. "*Resistance* leader."

"Not resistant enough, apparently, if you let these guys talk you into feeding them again."

The smile he won from her was still thin, but it lasted longer.

"Geez," Kat said. "Listen to them. They even sound like an old married couple."

Clint leaned over and helped himself to a buttery biscuit. "Nope. If they were an old married couple, the only sound you'd be hearing right now is a deafening silence."

"Cynic."

"Realist."

The familiar chatter felt oddly reassuring to Del. He waited for Bull to take a swallow of coffee and set down his mug. "You get anything off the phone records from the bar?"

The captain's jaw hardened. "Couldn't get the warrant signed."

"Can you believe that?" Kat piped in. "Even Gene tried. Every one of the judges—"

"Kat." Bull scowled at the junior ranger. Seemed to be his perpetual expression when she was around.

"Pressure's coming from high up on this," Gene said. "Even I couldn't get around it. I'm sorry."

Del tried to nod, but his muscles wouldn't cooperate. He ended up jerking his head to the side as he strode toward the bedroom in uneven steps. "Not your fault."

That was that, then. Their last lead—last hope—a dead end. An odd sense of detachment settled over him. He knew he should be disappointed or angry or scared, but all he could think about was a shower.

Long and wet and hot enough to peel skin.

The water ran a long time.

Elisa finished drying the breakfast dishes and paced the hallway between the living room and bedroom, unsure whether or not to go to Del. Uncertain what she would say if she did.

That same uncertainty eventually drove her to him. Much had changed between them in the past few days. They had become closer. Last night they might have become lovers if the police had not intervened.

But they had intervened. Del had been arrested, treated like a criminal. She knew law enforcement here was not as barbaric as Colonel Sanchez's tyranny in San Ynez. Prisoners here had rights.

But she also knew Del was a proud and honorable man. Being jailed by men he once considered friends, once stood beside to uphold the very laws under which he'd been accused, could not have been easy for him.

She hurt to think she bore responsibility for his heartache. If he had not married her, he would not be in this trouble.

Where did that leave their growing relationship?

Needing to know what he was thinking, she ducked into the tiny bathroom. Steam curled in the air like storm clouds rolling down a mountain valley. Water drummed like distant thunder.

Elisa sat on the lid to the john. Biting her lip, she twisted the plain gold band around her ring finger. "It will not help," she finally said.

The sloshing sounds inside the shower stilled. "Help what?"

"You can stand under the spray until you drown. Soap and water cannot wash away the humiliation of being treated like a criminal." She spoke from experience.

The faucet handles squeaked. The water stopped running and the shower door cracked open. The ranger held out his hand. "Give me a towel, would you?"

She pulled a thick, navy-blue bath towel from the rack and gave it to him, then turned her gaze away, but caught a flash of bronze skin through the condensation on the mirror.

A moment later, he stepped out of the shower stall. Water plastered his dark hair to his scalp and ran in rivulets over the bands of muscle bunched in his heavy shoulders. The blue towel clung low over his lean hips.

"What do you know about humiliation?" he asked.

When Elisa was able to pull her gaze away from the dark tunnel of navel that drilled into an abdomen as hard as concrete, and the arrow of hair between it and the top edge of the towel, she noticed he was frowning. The stubble on his unshaven jaw cast a fierce shadow on his expression.

He was spoiling for a fight.

"I have been called a traitor by my own government."

"A government you don't recognize as legitimate. To your people you're a hero. You're legendary."

"Not as legendary as the Texas Rangers."

"I'm not a ranger anymore, am I? I'm just a careless ex-cop who murdered an innocent man."

"Not so innocent, maybe. And you were right to protect your friend. It was not murder."

"Try telling that to the press. I'm sure it'll sound real convincing coming from the woman who married me a week after I killed her fiancé."

He turned his back on her, and it was like lighting a match to tinder. She followed him into the bedroom. "The press will not decide your guilt or innocence."

He stopped at his bureau and opened his underwear drawer. "If you believe that, darlin', you've got a lot to learn about life in the U.S. of A."

"Why wait until the day after tomorrow, then? Why not go to the judge now and plead guilty? Maybe if you beg the court for mercy they will find a hole to throw you in that is deep enough to hold you and all your self-pity."

He slammed the wooden drawer shut and wheeled. One step toward her put him close enough for her to smell the fresh, male scent of his soap, feel the moist heat rising from him. "Is that how you think I feel? Sorry for myself?"

"You walk around like a zombie. You let the police take you last night without even defending yourself. Your friends try to help and you send them away."

"I'm tired. Those street cops last night were just following orders. Arguing with them would have been pointless—and could have gotten somebody hurt. And my friends have risked enough already.''

''So you are giving up?''

''No. I'm fighting back.''

''How? I do not understand.''

''By not letting them send you back. No matter what they do to me.''

Elisa felt as if the breath had been vacuumed out of her. ''You are…protecting me?''

''I said I would.''

''You cannot go to jail because of me.''

''Apparently, I can,'' he said dryly.

''But last night…'' Last night he told her everything would be all right, and she had foolishly believed him.

''Last night I wanted to bring you back here and make love to you more than anything in the world. Of everything that's happened in the last few days, what I regret most is that I missed that chance.''

Elisa was stunned into silence. Tears welled up in her eyes. No one had ever made her feel so cherished with one simple confession.

While she was searching for the words to tell him so, his mouth descended on hers and she forgot everything but the feel of his kiss. With a nibble and a nudge, he coaxed her lips to play, enticed her tongue into the game with a darting probe and retreat. His hands swept into her hair, fisted.

Guided backward by the force of his hard body, Elisa backed up until the edge of the mattress bumped the creases behind her knees. Then she felt herself falling, being caught. She lost contact with his mouth, reached out for it desperately, bouncing between the bed and the impenetrable wall of his chest when he landed on top of her, cushioned by his elbows from crushing her.

His weight on her awakened nerve endings from her toes to her ears. Her body hummed, nearly sang when he took her lips again. Elisa arched, lifted herself into him, against his chest and his hips, which she'd become acutely aware were covered only by a thin, damp towel.

Deepening the kiss, he moaned deep in his throat. She stroked his back, relishing the feel of every inch of his firm flesh. His stubble scraped her cheek. There was nothing soft about the ranger. Nothing weak. The hard press of his body to hers made her wonder how she had ever imagined him capable of wallowing in self-pity. He knew exactly what he was doing, protecting his friends. Protecting her.

And she couldn't let him do it.

She wrenched her mouth away from his, turned her head to the side. Their harsh breathing filled the gulf of silence between them.

Slowly she turned her head back. "Last night was not our last. There will be other opportunities."

His gray eyes dulled. "But not today."

"Not when it feels like I'm trading it for your freedom."

He rolled off the bed and to his feet in one smooth move. Before she realized what he was doing, he grabbed the boxers he'd left atop his bureau, and the towel that had been around his hips fluttered to the floor. He stepped into his underwear with his back to her, but not before she caught an eyeful—two eyes full—of smooth, taut, beautiful male body.

He seemed unconcerned with her appraisal. "If you figure out a way to sleep with me without wrecking your moral code, let me know." He snatched a T-shirt from the bureau's second drawer. "Just don't wait too long. I figure this is going to be a speedy trial."

She sat on the edge of the bed. "A speedy farce, you mean. You know this is not about what happened at the warehouse."

"What do you want me to do? Start a rebellion? Build a bunker on some old farm, stockpile guns and declare the land a sovereign nation? It's been tried before. Doesn't work."

On shaky legs, Elisa walked to the living room and picked up a picture. The photograph depicted a group of weathered cowboys on horseback—late nineteenth-century era rangers—with heavy mustaches and long-barreled rifles.

She took the picture to Del.

Glancing down, he raised his eyebrows. "You want me to grow a bad mustache?"

"Read the caption."

"'They were men who could not be stampeded.'"

"That is what I want from you."

He handed the wooden frame back to her. "I told you, I'm not a ranger anymore."

She studied the grainy photo again, the creased faces, the familiar hard eyes. "I think you've been a ranger all your life and you always will be, whether you wear a silver star or not."

He took the wooden frame from her and set it on his dresser, then studied her a long time. Then he tweaked the front of her T-shirt and pulled her to him. "Anybody besides me ever tell you you're the most stubborn, infuriating woman they've ever met?"

"Almost everyone."

"I don't suppose you have a plan for how to pull off this miracle?"

A spark of hope kicked her pulse up. "I handled the motivation. Planning is your job." She arched one eyebrow, reading the glint in his eyes. "You do have a plan, don't you?"

"The woman from the bar," he admitted grudgingly.

Finally something clicked in Elisa's mind. "She called him 'Lalo.'"

"What?"

"Lalo. It is the Spanish nickname for Eduardo. Usually only used by family and friends. Very close friends."

"Maybe we questioned the wrong person at the bar," Del admitted.

"Maybe."

"You were planning to talk to her all along."

"Maybe," Del said.

Elisa jabbed a fist in his shoulder and handed him his shirt, then he tweaked the front of it once he had it on, pulling him to her. "Anybody besides me ever tell you you're the most stubborn, infuriating man they've ever met?"

He only grinned.

"Knew you'd be back." Dusty Partrain, lone waitress at The Last Buck, lit a cigarette with shaky hands and threw the smoldering match into an empty soda can on her kitchen table. The bar didn't open for another hour and a half, so Del and Elisa had tracked her to the address Clint pulled from the Department of Motor Vehicles.

"What makes you say that?" Del asked.

"I know cops."

"Been in trouble with the law before?"

She took a drag from her cigarette, puffed out her

lower lip and blew the smoke upward. It was almost 11:00 a.m., but she was wearing a bathrobe and her bleached-blond hair had not been washed.

She'd been pretty once, Del imagined, trying to see past the fatigue and hard living. Not a classic beauty like Elisa, but attractive in a down-home kind of way.

He wondered what had changed her.

"Once or twice," she finally answered. "Lalo always was after me to clean up my act. That's who you're here about, ain't it? Lalo?"

Del nodded, though he didn't like the way the woman kept glancing furtively at Elisa, or the way tremors in her hands had worsened and her breathing shallowed out.

"You knew Eduardo well," he said.

Another peek at Elisa. "Well enough."

"You called him Lalo. That's a nickname usually only used by family and close friends."

"I guess you could say that. Yeah. We were…close friends."

"How did you meet."

"I tried to trick him."

Elisa frowned. "Trick?"

"You're a prostitute?" Del asked, as much to clue in Elisa as to get an answer.

"I was. I tried to trick him, but he turned me down. Came back the next night, though, and took me to a hotel. I figured he was same as all the rest. But he didn't want nothing. Wouldn't take nothing from me."

Dusty's eyes filled. Her nasal passages clogged and she sniffed loudly. Del handed her a napkin from the duck-shaped napkin holder in the center of the Formica table. "Not for months, anyway. Till after I got off the drugs and alcohol and got a reg'lar job at the bar."

Elisa stiffened. Del cursed himself silently. He should

have known. Damn it, he should have taken one look at Dusty Partrain and known she'd been Garcia's lover. The woman's loss was written all over her stooped shoulders, her sad eyes.

Dusty wiped her nose with the wadded napkin. "That was all before, 'course."

Del noted uneasily the ramrod set to Elisa's spine, the lack of color in her cheeks. It had to hurt to hear that Eduardo had another lover. He wanted to get her out of there, but the stubborn slant to her jaw was enough to convince him she wasn't leaving without her answers.

"Before what?" Elisa asked, as if to prove the point.

"Before you," Dusty said sadly. "Least before he got the letter about that baby you're carrying."

Del stood. That was it. He was getting her out of here. "'Lis, why don't we step outside a minute?"

As usual she ignored him. "He told you about the baby?"

"He broke it off with me. After three years, he ended it just like it was nothing." Dusty's lower lip wobbled, but she held back the new tears. "Said he couldn't marry me like we planned because he had to marry you. It was the *right thing to do.*"

Well, hell. He was ending this. Now. Staring at the toes of his ostrich-skin boots, he asked, "Dusty, do you know anything about what happened at the warehouse the day Eduardo was killed?"

He expected a quick no. That would be that, and he could take Elisa and go. What he got was a hiccup, then a sobbing woman. Hesitantly—and amazingly, given that she had just found out the woman had been her fiancé's lover—Elisa rubbed Dusty's back.

"He'd been working on that deal for months," Dusty choked out. "Said everything depended on it. I didn't know what it was about, until the night he told me about…he said he was marrying someone else. We had a fight, but he ended up staying over one last time.'' She glanced at Elisa, bit her lip and continued. ''I heard him use the phone when he thought I was asleep. He talked about guns and colonel somebody or other.''

''Sanchez?''

''Maybe that was it. I…I don't remember. He said they'd make the deal in three days, on Monday.''

''Son of a bitch,'' Del exclaimed. Not because they had proof Eduardo was dealing guns, but because the man had waited until three days before Elisa's arrival to break off his relationship with his girlfriend, and even then he'd *stayed over* one last time.

Dusty took another cigarette from her pack, but didn't light it. ''The next morning I begged him not to go. He didn't want to—it was tearing him up, I could see it. But he said he had to. I was mad. Hurt. I didn't understand. I wanted to hurt him—''

She stopped for a breath. ''So Monday morning I called the Texas Rangers and told them about the guns.'' Her face crumpled like the tissue in her fist. ''Now Lalo is dead. It's my fault.''

The anonymous tipster. The pieces were all falling into place now. The jilted lover had tried to screw up Eduardo's deal in retribution. She hadn't realized it could kill him. Afterward, she'd been too broken up by guilt to tell anyone. Since the incoming phone calls at the ranger office weren't routinely recorded, there had been no way to connect her to the call.

Del sighed, not sure where to go next. Not sure if there was anywhere *to* go. He could haul Dusty into court, force her to testify that Eduardo had been involved in the gun deal in the warehouse, but what good would it do? She was a former drug addict and prostitute. The prosecution would tear her to shreds.

He was ready to leave. More than ready. They hadn't accomplished anything here other than to further disillusion Elisa about the man she'd intended to marry. Only, Elisa didn't seem so anxious to take off. She had pulled Dusty's head to her shoulder and was rocking the woman, whispering words of solace.

One final possibility occurred to Del. It was a long shot, but worth asking. "Ms. Partrain, you said Eduardo used your phone. Have you received this month's bill yet, by any chance?"

Wiping her eyes with the back of her hand, Dusty nodded. She pulled out of Elisa's embrace and retrieved an envelope from a particle-board desk in the living room.

Del scanned the itemized call list, automatically stopping at the number prefixed by area code 202.

Washington, D.C.

Heart quickening, he pulled the cell phone off his belt and punched in the number. He held his breath when someone picked up. A silky female voice answered, "U.S. State Department. How may I direct your call?"

Chapter 14

"You're sending me away?" Sinking against the headboard of Del's bed, she watched as he swooped around the room, gathering the belongings she'd collected in her weeks with him and shoving them into a small black suitcase with wheels. His energy made her even more tired than the morning's revelations. She was ready for her afternoon nap, but Del didn't seem inclined to let her have it.

"Clint is going to get you to Canada. He'll set you up there with a new name. He knows how. I've already called the bank. They'll have five thousand dollars cash and a cashier's check for the balance of my accounts waiting for you."

Bitter disappointment washed the back of her throat. They had come so far together, become so much more than they had been—strangers thrown together by an impossible circumstance. Foolishly, she had dared hope there was more for them yet.

She had fallen in love with him.

"And if I do not want to go?" she asked.

He yanked open a bureau drawer and hurled a stack of underwear toward the open bag. He was like a laser— a pure, focused stream of energy. And hot enough to burn. Barely controlled fury radiated from him in waves. "Don't you get it? If Eduardo was making calls to the State Department, then they knew what he was doing. The U.S. Government is selling weapons to Colonel Sanchez."

"Perhaps Eduardo called to warn your government of the deal."

"Then why weren't there federal agents all over that warehouse?"

"Maybe they did not believe him."

"Doubt it. Since September 11, they tend to take that kind of thing very seriously."

"Yet they would sell guns to a country that supports terrorists?"

"They may not know as much about Sanchez as you do. Or maybe they think they can use him as an informant, or that they can buy his loyalty and get him to squeeze the terrorists out. Wouldn't be the first time the U.S. did something like this. Ever hear of Iran-Contra?"

"I studied economics, not politics."

"Then you understand one thing. Profit. In the end, none of them care about people getting shot in the streets or blown up in their own homes. It's all about making a buck."

"Not for everyone."

"All but a rare few."

"Like you."

He stopped packing long enough look at her, finally.

"I'm no saint, Elisa. You, more than anyone, know that."

"You have already punished yourself for Eduardo's death more harshly than any court could." She stood, brushed her knuckles across his rough jaw and found herself swaying toward him, pulled to him without conscious will. "Is that why you are sending me away? To punish yourself?"

"Eduardo's accomplices in the State Department are worried about what he might have told you. For all they know, you could blow the lid off their whole conspiracy. If they can't force you out of the country through a legal deportation, they might try to get rid of you…another way. It's dangerous for you to stay here."

"It is dangerous for you also. You are the one about to go on trial. If these men can have you arrested, can they not also tamper with your trial? Ensure you are convicted?"

"They would have to convince twelve people. A jury of my peers."

"You do not think this is possible?" Even with her limited knowledge of American politics and the legal system, she knew better.

"I can take care of myself."

"You can. But will you? Or will you let them lock you away so that I can go free?"

"I'm not going down without a fight, if that's what you mean. But I can't take these guys on if I'm worried about you."

"You do not know who is involved or how high up the corruption goes. What kind of chance—" Elisa didn't have to finish the question. She knew what kind of chance he had against them—about as much chance as a snowstorm in the jungle.

A chill not even his fire could warm seeped into her bones. If the conspirators, whoever they were, were willing to get rid of her "another way," might they also be willing to get rid of him another way? A single bullet was much more certain than an attempt to sway twelve people. "You must let me go."

"That's what I'm doing."

"Not to Canada. Back to San Ynez."

"Are you nuts?"

"You must dissolve the marriage. Divorce me, and let them deport me."

"No way."

"It is the only way."

"You can't go back there."

"My people will protect me." They would, to the best of their ability. But it would not be enough against Sanchez's soldiers. She had thought the United States would be her refuge. Finally she accepted she could not hide from fate. With her eyes tearing, her hand curved sadly over the mound of her abdomen. She had wanted so much for the little one. It just was not meant to be.

The ranger's jaw set. "No."

What was left of Elisa's pride held her back straight and her head high. She could not let him do this. "Then I will divorce you."

"Like hell."

"I cannot let you sacrifice your freedom, possibly your life, for me."

"I told you I'm no saint, Elisa. I'm not doing this for you. I'm doing this for me. Because I wanted you from the moment I laid eyes on you, even though I knew it was wrong. Even though I thought you were in love with another man. A dead man."

"You...you wanted—"

''I told myself I was only helping you because I owed you, and for the baby's sake. I lied.''

Blood pounded in Elisa's ears until she had to strain to hear his words.

''You're the most beautiful woman I've ever seen, Elisa. I wanted to look at you twenty-four hours a day. I wanted to hear your voice in the morning and smell you in the evening.''

''Sm-smell me?''

''You smell like vanilla and almonds. It drives me crazy. So I told myself I could see you and hear you and smell you, but I'd keep my hands off you. I lied about that, too.''

''I...I like your hands on me.''

''I'm a selfish, greedy bastard. I wanted you. Now I've got you, and by God, I'm not giving up what's *mine*.''

The last word shuddered out in a possessive growl, and all her reasons why she should not make love to him ticked away like seconds on a clock, never to be recaptured. Her knees went as weak as her will. If he had not caught her, she would have fallen. He did catch her, though, and he lifted her up as if she were weightless. Even when he laid her on the bed, she felt herself drifting like a dust mote in the light, nothing holding her but air and his arms.

His knee nudged her legs apart, and his hard thighs settled home between hers. He held his weight off her with his elbows. ''I want you Elisa. But I have to know there's no one in this bed but you and me. No ghosts. Because I couldn't live with myself if I made love to you when you still blamed me for Eduardo's death. If you do, tell me to stop now, while I still can.''

''I do not want you to stop.'' Her arms circled his back, which rose and fell in time with his rough breaths.

"Then tell me you'll go to Canada."

"I will think about going to Canada. Tomorrow."

"And today?"

"Today I am counting on you to take me someplace else, entirely." She raised one knee between his legs, caressed him intimately, and his eyes darkened in surrender.

"You might have to help me." One of his hands left the bed to smooth over her ribs and rest on her swollen womb. "I'm not familiar with the terrain around here."

"Nothing you could do would hurt me or the baby."

"Just to make sure, how about we take it slow and easy?" His wandering hand moved lower, grazing her hip and the delta of her thighs.

Elisa bit her lip. "How slow?"

"This slow." He lowered his head and laved his tongue over the tender spot behind her ear in a long, lazy stroke. "And this slow." His blunt fingers traced a circle on her breast, teasingly close to, but not quite touching, the nipple that ached for his touch.

"Have I ever told you." She had to stop talking to breathe. She had never felt so engulfed by a man. So enveloped in sensation by the slightest touch. "That in San Ynez I have a reputation as being somewhat impatient?"

A Cheshire smile scrolled across his face. "I would never have guessed."

"I can be downright over-eager at times." She reached for the hem of his T-shirt, but he bucked away.

"Downright? You're starting to sound like a Texan."

"Yes? How about this? I'm fixin' to rope and tie you if you don't git back down here."

He laughed. "Now you sound like you're from Fort Worth." His laughter stopped and he leaned close. Storm clouds churned in his gray eyes, whipping the gentle breeze that had been holding her aloft into gales. ''I'll let you tie me up later, if you want. How about we stick with freestyle for now?''

This time when she reached for his shirt, he let her strip him. Then he opened the top of her sundress, lingering over each pearly button until they were both naked from the waist up.

Elisa swallowed hard. She had seen his chest before. But never looming over her. Never so close she could feel the solid thump of his heart in her own blood. Touch the steely mass of muscle or the smooth, hot skin. He burned like he had a fever. A fever for her.

Awed, she pressed her palm to his sternum. When she came to the U.S., she had thought she was giving up her independence, commissioning her future into the hands of a man she barely knew. When that man was killed and she accepted the ranger's help, she thought she sacrificed her pride as well.

Knowing he wanted her with such ferocity restored a bit of her self-regard. It also made her feel she had some control over her destiny. Bravely she took his hand and pressed his big fingers to her breast. He let her set the pressure and rhythm a moment, then took over when she drew her hand away.

Leaning over her, he whispered. ''Is this how you like to be touched?''

She nodded, losing coherency.

One-handed, he freed the remaining buttons on her sundress and pushed back the flaps. His knuckles brushed the line below her white cotton panties, tickling the tender crease just inside her hip where leg meets torso. Her stomach muscles fluttered.

''And this?'' he said, his voice getting rougher.

She nodded again, head thrown back while his magic hands levitated her. Higher and higher she floated until, mewling, she reached for the snap of his jeans. She got them unfastened, but he pulled away, denying her the contact she sought. He stood, shucking the jeans and boxers, then helped her wriggle out of her panties. The process allowed her more than enough time to realize that the parts of him she had not seen were every bit as magnificent as the parts she had. A tingle of anticipation buzzed along her nerves as he lowered his full, naked length to her. Hands thrown over her head, she arched into his male hardness and heat. His strong arms supported her while his fingers penetrated her and she was flying with him. Soaring.

How could she ever have thought of marriage to him as a sacrifice? It was a gift.

He rolled with her, settling her on top, and she realized he was every breath she took. He set her free.

Elisa had never been skydiving before, but she imagined this was how it must feel. Balancing over the ranger's flushed, naked body, she felt as if she were teetering on the brink of a plane's open hatch, looking out at a mile of nothingness between her feet and the earth.

Their gazes met, held, and without hesitation she leaped.

His hands on her hips guided her gently down. She tipped her head back, focused on the expansion of her body, nearly grimacing with the strain of accommodation.

"Don't…let…me…hurt you," he ground out, but she barely heard him with the winds of passion rushing by her, roaring in her ears.

Touching the tip of her tongue to her upper lip in concentration, she angled her hips a few degrees and pressed down. With a pop, the pressure inside her released, and she seated herself fully on him.

For a moment they did nothing more than breathe—it was all either of them could manage. Then he took her hands in his and brought them to his chest, tilting her forward. Slowly his hips lifted her, pushing him deeper inside her. Hipbone to hipbone they gyrated, and then floated back to the bed. Her thighs tightened, held him, and he took her back up again. And again.

They moved harder. Gasped louder. The mattress squeaked. The headboard rapped the wall. Del reached for her breasts, plumped and squeezed them, shooting a molten message straight to her core. Her fists twisted in the sheets. Her hair hung over them like a curtain, tangling in his hands. Tied together, they flew. Soared.

"That's perfect. You're perfect," he said through gritted teeth, punctuating each word with an upward thrust. "I love you."

The unexpected declaration sent her spiraling out of control. Never had she felt like this. She was free-falling. Diving headlong into oblivion. She twisted, grasping at air, gasping for breath from the greedy wind rushing by. Vertigo took her in its grip and she couldn't tell down from up, right from left. The world was spinning, her body was convulsing and the scream that pierced the roar of the wind sounded like her own.

When she regained her balance, she was lying on his chest. Del's body was arched and tight as a strung bow until his own release subsided and he sagged beneath her.

He smoothed back the long, black hair plastered to both their faces.

"What," she asked, still disoriented, "was that?"

He smiled lazily. "That, sweetheart, was one more

reason to fight the bastards that want to keep us apart, until my last breath.''

"Clint will take you to the train station," Del told Elisa the next morning. Ranger Clint Hayes followed the discussion by watching in the rearview mirror. "He'll put you on a rail to Detroit, then catch a plane and meet you there. He'll help you get over the border and stay with you until you're settled."

When he was through repeating the plan for the tenth time, Del couldn't quite meet Elisa's gaze. Instead he stared out the back window of his Land Rover at DuPage Street, a block away from the Dallas County Courthouse, where his arraignment was scheduled to begin in half an hour.

Elisa sat as stiff as a mannequin in the seat next to him. "You cannot go to the courthouse."

"I have to."

"You said you were going to fight." Her voice crackled like fire on dry tinder.

Del sighed. He shouldn't have left this for the last minute. He should have said goodbye at home. Or slipped out of bed this morning before she woke. God knew, he tried.

He met Clint's gaze in the mirror. "Give us a minute?"

With a sympathetic nod, Clint stepped out of the vehicle and closed the driver's door behind him.

"I am going to fight. But *through* the system."

Her head snapped toward him. Her gaze was sharp as a buck knife. "The same system that sells guns to an army run by a madman?"

"The system I've spent my whole life upholding." It tore him up to think his country might be responsible for any of the suffering in San Ynez. But he still couldn't turn his back on the American way.

She popped the car door open, stepped into the street. A car blared its horn at her as it swerved to the center lane. More deliberately he followed, and joined her on the bench at a bus stop a few yards away.

"You could come with me to Canada," she said.

"And abandon my family?"

"You would rather have them visit you in prison?"

He shook his head slowly. What would his grandfather say? His father? He didn't know. He did know one thing. "I'm supposed to be one of the good guys, 'Lis. I can't live as a fugitive. I just don't have it in me."

"And I would rather die than live with that kind of injustice."

He kicked a pebble, and a pigeon scrabbled after it as if it were a breadcrumb. He felt bad for giving the bird false hopes. "I guess we'll always be on opposite sides of the coin on that one."

She stared at the cement between her sandals. "You said you loved me. Was it just…the moment? Or did you mean it?"

He tipped her head up to his with his hand on her chin. Del had never thought twice about the term *broken heart*. He figured it was just a romantic notion for love-struck teenage girls. After today he might have to revise that assumption. Because when he lifted Elisa's head and saw the tears glistening in her eyes, it felt like someone had stuck a handsaw in his chest and was hacking away.

"I never say what I don't mean," he told her, willing her to believe it. "Especially that."

"I…I love you, too."

A grin tried to crack on his face even as his heart fell

into two neat halves. "I was wondering when you were going to work up the nerve to tell me."

She jerked her chin away.

Clint walked toward them. He didn't say anything, and his eyes were hidden by mirrored shades, but a tap on his watch told Del what was on his mind. Del would be late if he didn't get moving.

He pulled Elisa to her feet and put her in the front passenger seat, lowering the power window and leaning in as he shut the door between them. "Even if they convict me, they can't lock me up forever. When I get out, I'll come for you."

"Do not make promises you might not be able to keep."

He hardly let her finish her complaint before he crushed his mouth over hers. Damn it, he hadn't meant to kiss her. He'd meant to make a clean break. Say his goodbyes and walk away, even if it killed him.

They'd left his bed only a few hours ago, and already his body was hungry for hers again. His need for her was a physical craving. Only, it wasn't just the physical release he craved. The moment she was out of earshot he longed to hear her voice; the moment she slid out of his grasp he longed to feel her again; the moment a kiss ended he longed to taste her again.

He was the man who had pledged to help her, the Texas Ranger, and yet somehow he'd come to depend on her strength. Her resolve.

Damn, but she wasn't even gone and already he ached for her.

He broke off the kiss before it was too late, before he couldn't walk away at all, and thumped his palm on the roof of the car to signal Clint to go. "Wherever you are,'' he said, focusing all his will, all his strength into that one sure statement, ''I'll find you.''

The first of her tears rolled down her cheek. Even with all she had been through, this was the first time he'd seen her cry, Del realized.

She shook her head, then looked at him through glazed, wet eyes. Her head tilted as if something were broken inside her. ''You were right before. We do not believe in the same things. We are too different.''

The car rolled forward a foot. Del kept pace on the curb, his face twisting. '''Lis? No. *I will find you.*''

She looked over her shoulder as the Rover pulled into traffic. ''It would better for us both if you did not.''

How many blocks passed before she reined in her emotions, Elisa could not be sure. What she was sure of, was that Clint Hayes scowled at her through every one of them.

''Damn women,'' he mumbled, his hands strangling the steering wheel. ''Ought to be a law against 'em.''

''I am sorry,'' she said, though she was not sure what she was apologizing for, other than being female. And maybe for whatever woman had ruined his opinion of the gender.

''Damn well ought to be sorry,'' he said, spearing her with a hard look. ''You didn't have to do that, you know?''

''Do what?''

''Rip Del up. Leave him in pieces after everything he's done for you.''

She squirmed deeper in the bucket seat. ''I did not ask for his help.''

''How about sex, did you ask him for that? He'd already given you his name, a ring and every penny he had, but you had to seduce him, too. Make sure he had nothing left when you were gone, not even his self-respect.''

Clint's anger knocked the breath out of her. ''I did not seduce—''

But she had known Del well enough to realize that once they made love, his commitment to her would grow even deeper. She would not be just the woman to whom he owed a debt. She would be his wife, in every sense of the word. He would not do anything to jeopardize her safety.

Even save himself.

''I am sorry,'' she said again, and this time she meant it.

''Aw.'' Clint waved his hand impotently. ''Wouldn't have goddamn mattered. Damn Del, it's like he's got this code of honor of his hardwired in his brain.''

The last honorable man, she had once thought of him. She had been right.

''Please take me to the courthouse.''

''You've got a train to catch.''

''I need to say goodbye properly.'' She could feel him appraising her from behind his mirrored lenses. ''He deserves better, but it is the best I can do.''

At the next corner Clint swung the Land Rover in wide U-turn. ''So help me, lady, you do right by him this time or I'll put you on a plane to San Ynez myself.''

They hurried through the parking garage at the courthouse, counting the minutes before Del's case was called. At the elevator Clint punched the up button and checked his watch. ''Fifteen minutes. We'll make it.''

She nodded and nervously watched the lights indicating the elevator's descent to their level. She had no idea what she would say when she found Del. If he would even talk to her.

The last light blinked on, a bell dinged and the lift doors opened. Before she and Clint could step on, a man stepped out of the stairwell to her right, pulling a deadly looking pistol from beneath his sport coat.

Clint shoved her to the floor with one hand and reached for the gun at his hip with the other. A shot exploded, echoing like thunder through the concrete garage, and Clint hit the ground rolling, blood already spreading across his left shoulder. His gun clattered to the cement beside Elisa. She picked it up, and the shooter dived for the cover of a steel drum being used as a traffic barricade. Before he could set up for another shot, Elisa dragged Clint behind the minivan in the parking space next to them.

She was searching for something to stanch the flow of blood from Clint's arm when cold metal touched her temple. A second man stepped out from behind her.

Knowing it was useless, she instinctively raised the ranger's gun a fraction of an inch. The first man appeared, smiling, and kicked it from her hand. "I don't think so, sweetheart. Move away from ranger-boy. You're coming with us."

Chapter 15

The fifteen steps to the front entrance to the Dallas County Courthouse looked like Mt. Everest to Del. He dreaded the climb. Loathed the pack of reporters that waited for him at the glass doors like feral dogs at a rabbit hole.

With a deep breath he focused on his goal—get in, enter his plea, get out—and started forward. Standing here broiling in the sun wasn't going to help.

"Ranger Cooper, you've been charged with negligent homicide. What do you have to say?"

"Ranger Cooper, how will you plead?"

Never slowing his forward momentum, he shoved a microphone out of his face. "Haven't you people figured it out yet? I'm not a Texas Ranger anymore."

The burly anchor for Channel Seven blocked his path. "*Mr.* Cooper, how will you plead when your case is called?"

"Guilty on a charge of assault and battery if you don't get out of my way."

A dozen lights flashed in his face. Half the news crews walked away. They'd gotten their sound bite for the noon report. On to ruin someone else's day.

Del pushed through the dispersing crowd into the cool lobby and through the security checkpoint. Turning the last corner before he reached his assigned check-in area, his stomach dropped. His grandparents sat rigidly on a hard wooden bench. Dressed in their church clothes, they looked older and grayer than when he'd seen them just a few days ago.

His steps slowed. He fought a childish urge to turn and run the other way like he had when he'd been seven years old and left the gate to the chicken coop open. The coyotes had taken three of Mami's best hens.

It wasn't fear that fueled his apprehension over facing his grandparents with his failure all those years ago. Nor was it now. They would never hurt him or stop loving him.

Shame was what held him back. Deep and raw remorse.

Bad enough he'd left the Rangers in disgrace. Been branded a criminal. But to have his grandparents in the court when the charges were read against him…that would be worse than the rest combined.

Seeing his grandparents disappointed had always hurt Del more than any physical punishment could.

They stood when they saw him. *"Querido,"* Mami crooned, her hand brushing his cheek and a tear in her eye.

"You shouldn't have come."

"We wouldn't be anywhere else," his grandfather

said. "Jury can see what kind of person a man is by what kind of family he's from."

"This is just an arraignment. The judge will read the charges, I'll enter my plea and they'll set a court date. No jury."

"*Querido,* you said your rangers agreed that you did nothing wrong. This Garcia's death, it was an accident."

He shuffled foot to foot. The last thing he wanted to do was get into a discussion about what was really happening here in the courthouse hallway. "Things have gotten a little complicated. There are more people involved, not just rangers. Nothing is exactly what it seems."

Papi thumped his cane on the floor. "What does that mean?"

Del shifted his gaze left and right to see who might be watching. Or listening. "I can't explain right now. Please, just go on home. Mom will be worried, being there alone. I'll come by as soon as I can and fill you in."

"I don't like this, son. Not one bit."

"I know, Pap. But I have to go check in before they call my case. Please. Take Mami home."

Walking away from his grandparents was almost as hard as watching Elisa drive away. His chest felt as if it had been filled with concrete, and a lump the size of Amarillo rose in his throat. He almost went back to them, realizing he hadn't told them he loved them, but he only had nine minutes before his case was called.

He laid his hand on the door to the room where his lawyer was supposed to be waiting to check him in. A siren screamed by outside, close. His ears tuned it in a second before he chastised himself for caring. He wasn't a cop anymore.

Someone clapped his shoulder from behind.

Del turned. The cement in his chest settled lower. "You son of a bitch. Who are you?"

Mr. Baseball, dressed today in a conservative pinstripe and carrying a briefcase, nodded down the hall.

"I'm not going anywhere with you until you tell me who you are."

The man sauntered away, whistling. "I'm the man who just might be able to make your life worth living again." He turned in a small conference room two doors down.

Del checked his watch. Eight minutes. Swearing, he followed Mr. Mysterious. The man made himself comfortable at the conference room table, setting a file folder out in front of him.

"Nothing more," Del said, "until I know who you are."

The man straightened his tie. "You can call me Mr. Bradford."

"Who do you work for?"

"The same person who used to employ you, only at a higher level. Uncle Sam."

"Could you be more specific?"

"Do you want to play twenty questions, or do you want me to tell you how you can walk into that courtroom in—" he checked his watch "—seven minutes and clear your name."

"What are you going to do? Buy another judge?"

"I don't have to." The man shoved the file across the table to Del.

Reluctantly Del sat, opened it and started reading.

"Since you're running short on time, I'll save you the trouble of reading. It's a deposition signed by a federal agent saying that you didn't kill Eduardo Garcia."

Del's stomach bounced off the floor of his abdomen. He looked up, speechless, then back down to the folder to confirm.

"We had a mole in the warehouse that day." Bradford, if that really was his name, smiled smugly at Del's disbelief. "Your tax dollars at work."

"If you had an undercover operative in there, how come you're just now sharing this information?"

"Our man was so deep we couldn't get a report from him until last night."

Del flipped a few pages in the deposition. "Eduardo was the middle man who set up the sale. The deal went bad, and the buyers tied him up and executed him. With a shotgun."

"Five minutes before the Texas Rangers arrived."

Del cocked his jaw. It was possible. "Buckshot can't be traced by ballistic matching, like a regular bullet."

"There was no way to know the blast that killed Garcia hadn't come from your weapon." The man shrugged. "Until now."

Del closed the folder, tapped his fingers on the cover. "It's a neat story."

"I thought you'd like it."

"Too neat."

The man leaned back in his chair. "If you don't want my help, I'll take my folder and go. If, on the other hand, you want to clear your name, you hand that to your lawyer and all charges will be dropped. The records will be sealed, of course. Classified. But your slate is cleared. I might even be able to put in a word with the DPS. Get you rehired."

He could have it all back. His reputation, his job. It seemed too good to be true. The trouble with things that seemed too good to be true is, they usually were.

Still, he wasn't ready to let go of the folder. "And Elisa?"

"Your wife's association with a gun smuggler makes her an undesirable in this country. Even marriage to a U.S. citizen can't prevent deportation of someone judged to be dangerous or involved in criminal activity."

Del shoved his chair back and stood. "She didn't know Eduardo was working for Sanchez."

"Is that what she told you?"

"That's what I know. Furthermore, if you had an operative in the warehouse, he wasn't a mole. If he was, he wouldn't have been there alone. He would have had cover for himself and that cache of weapons. And if he wasn't a mole, there's only one other explanation. He was selling guns to a foreign military. An activity the United States Congress seriously frowns upon. So yeah." He snatched the folder from the table. "I'll take your deposition and give it to my lawyer. We'll tell a story to the judge and all those nice reporters waiting outside. Only it might not be exactly the story you'd been hoping for. So, if I were you, I'd start worrying less about how I'm going to clear my name, and more about how you're going to clear yours."

He turned to leave.

"You're an idiot, Cooper. You can't win this. You're dealing with the highest levels of this country's government. *The highest.*"

"The higher they are, the farther they have to fall."

"You'd really throw away everything for a woman?"

He stopped. "No, I'd be hanging on to the one thing that matters more than my job, my name, even my freedom. My self-respect."

"I can have this whole thing taken out of here. Moved to a military tribunal."

He pulled the door open. Kat and Captain Matheson stood ten feet down the hallway. Sensing trouble, they shifted to ready stances.

Del looked over his shoulder. Mr. Baseball looked as if he'd spent too much time in the sun. His face was red, and he'd popped a sweat.

Turning back to the hall, he gave Bull and Kat a silent heads-up signal with a faint jerk of his chin. "You can try," he said to the man behind him as he walked out.

Kat and Bull flanked him on either side.

"What's going on?" Kat whispered.

"Hold it for later, Kat," Bull growled under his breath. Bradford's footfalls echoed on the tile floor behind them.

"Cooper, wait."

Grudgingly Del stopped and turned. His friends pulled up beside him, their duty faces on.

"We need to talk," the man said, dabbing at his forehead with a handkerchief. "Alone."

"There's nothing you could say that can't be said in front of my friends." He smiled. "Seein's how you all work for Uncle Sam."

The man's gaze flitted nervously over the rangers before settling on Del. "What I'm about to tell you is highly sensitive information."

"Get to the point."

Mr. Redface shoved his handkerchief into his back pocket. "You were right about the warehouse. Our operative was the one making the sale. But it wasn't real. It was a sting. Our man didn't have any cover because we had no intention of busting the buy, and we didn't want to risk his cover by having a bunch of cops around."

"What operative?" Kat asked, wide eyed. "What sting?"

Bull silenced her with a glare.

The man continued, uninterrupted. "Garcia was our in-country man. He made contact with Sanchez's people."

"Using a trip with the World-Aid Organization as his cover."

The man nodded, swallowed nervously. "He got Sanchez's men here, but we want the big kahuna himself."

"Sanchez?"

"We're going to extradite him—forcefully—from his own country the way we did Manuel Noriega in the early nineties. He's harboring terrorists—not to mention producing a hell of a lot of drugs that find their way onto American streets. We just needed concrete proof. We had tracking devices in the packing crates with the guns. All we had to do was get them in his hands, wait for him to resell them to the terrorists, then snap a few satellite shots of nice little homing blips coming from terrorist training camps, and we had him cold."

"So what happened?"

The man shook his head. "We don't know. Somehow they got wind he might be tied to the rebel faction in San Ynez."

"Resistance," Del corrected automatically. Then he closed his eyes. *"Elisa."*

If Sanchez's goons had found out Eduardo had a rebel—resistance—girlfriend, it would have cast doubt on his loyalty to the colonel. Except, the Fed here didn't seem to know she was a rebel.

"She's the wild card in all this. Details about her are sketchy at best. Her stumbling into Garcia's path just as he got wounded in San Ynez, forcing his care into her hands, might not have been an accident. Sanchez might have ordered her to cozy up to Eduardo to spy on him. For all we know, that baby she's carrying isn't really even his—''

Del grabbed the man by his lapels and pinned him to the wall. The other rangers calmed the passersby.

''Elisa doesn't have any connection to Sanchez,'' Del said. ''She couldn't. She's part of the resistance.'' He laughed. Finally, everything she stood for seemed so right to him. He knew what guilt she carried over her relationship with Eduardo. He couldn't wait to find her and tell her the father of her child hadn't been a traitor to his people after all, but a hero, as determined to stop Sanchez's reign of terror as she was. Maybe he could take a plane, be there to meet her train when it arrived in Detroit.

He laughed despite himself, filled with pride for her. ''Hell, she's La Puma, the leader of the whole damn resistance movement. Sanchez would execute her if he caught her.''

The man Del held blanched. ''Elisa Reyes is La Puma?''

''She was. Until she got pregnant and came to the United States to make a better life for her baby.''

''Oh, God.'' The man closed his eyes. ''I didn't know.''

Del's blood chilled. ''What?''

''My men saw her pull out of the parking garage ten minutes ago with two of Sanchez's goons.''

Elisa paced the walls of her eight-by-eight cell, digging at the windowsill, testing for weakness for the hundredth time and still finding none. As far as she could tell, she had been back in San Ynez, in this hole, three days, but she didn't know how long she'd been traveling before that. They drugged her, she thought. She didn't remember much of the trip.

She strode to the window and back again, her hand resting on her swollen belly. "It's all right, little one," she said. She'd taken to talking to the baby during her captivity. It reassured them both. "I got out of here once. I can do it again."

She wondered where Del was tonight. If he, too, was behind bars, or worse.

A key scraped against a metal lock, and the door clicked open. Elisa raised her hand to shield her eyes from the light spearing into the dim room. "Back for more questions, Colonel?"

His pocked face sneered at her. "This time I expect some answers." He slapped a baton against the palm of his hand. "I've been gentle with you so far out of respect for your...condition. But even my compassion has limits."

"Hopefully they are broader than the limits of your intelligence, because I have no idea what you want me to tell you."

"I want to know Eduardo Garcia's mission."

They had covered this ground before. She could only be thankful he seemed fixated on Eduardo and had not connected her to La Puma. If he had, no doubt she would be dead.

She had to stall until she could come up with an escape plan. Last night and the night before, she had denied any knowledge of a mission. The way he was cracking the baton against his hand, she doubted that would work again.

She decided on another tactic. One she hoped would gain her as much information as she gave away. "How would I know what his mission was?'' she asked, her lips thin. She felt shamed that she had been involved with a traitor. ''He worked for you.''

Sanchez paused midswing. ''You think Eduardo worked for me? How interesting.''

Thwack. The baton hit his palm.

''Eduardo Garcia was one of former Presidente Herrerra's personal bodyguards.''

Elisa's breath stalled. Eduardo? One of Herrerra's elite protection units? Those men had been the crown jewels of the San Ynez military when it was an honorable force. She could not believe one of them would turn on his countrymen.

Sanchez circled her with his baton. ''Now he offers to sell me guns. I want to know for what purpose.''

So did Elisa. ''What does it matter? He is dead.''

''Yes. It's unfortunate I had to have him killed, and leave all those lovely weapons behind. But I could not risk letting him live once I found out who he was.'' Sanchez tipped her chin up with the baton. ''And that he had taken a rebel lover.''

Elisa's heart tried to break out of her chest. He did not know who she was. He could not. Calming herself, she realized what the colonel had just said. ''You had him killed? But—''

A knock sounded on the door. A young soldier popped his head in and said breathlessly, ''Colonel—''

''Fool! I told you I did not want to be interrupted.''

''But, sir—''

With one step, Sanchez was at the door and rapped the baton on the boy's shoulder hard enough to snap bone. The boy writhed in pain. ''But, sir...we're under attack!''

* * *

Three dozen members of the San Ynez People's Resistance Movement—supported by an American infantry squad—fired into the air and generally raised a racket in front of the Sanchez compound while six special forces paratroopers—and one former paratrooper—parachuted inside the rear wall. Silently they gathered their black chutes and rigging and stuffed them behind bushes, then moved out across the compound. Though they could talk to each other with a mere whisper into the ultrasensitive micro-electronic headsets they each wore, they communicated only by hand signal, unwilling to risk announcing their arrival with even the slightest noise.

The main house was lit up like the castle at Disney World, and to give Elisa credit, it did look to Del a little like Gene Randolph's estate, except it was stucco instead of brick, and had a red tile roof instead of Gene's cedar-shingled one. Plus, Sanchez's mansion was about twice as large as the Randolph estate. Drug dealers lived in style these days.

Only one guard stood watch at the back door, and he wasn't very well trained. One of the paratroopers took him out so easily that he almost seemed disappointed the man hadn't put up more of a fight. It looked as if all the San Ynezian soldiers worth their salt had bought the diversion out front, as they were supposed to.

Inside, four of the paratroopers headed upstairs, to the office suite where Sanchez was likely to be. Del and one volunteer, the kid who had taken out the guard outside, went down, looking for Elisa.

They found her much more quickly than they'd anticipated. She stood at bottom of the stairs. Right behind her stood Colonel Sanchez, with a gun pointed at the swell in her belly that held her child.

The young paratrooper spoke excitedly into his headset when he should have been looking for cover. "Charlie One, Charlie One. I've got him. I've got Sanchez. Do you read?"

Sanchez swung the muzzle of his pistol away from Elisa momentarily, and fired. The paratrooper tumbled down the stairs, blood arcing from a wound in his neck.

"You've got no one," Sanchez said. His black eyes were dead calm. The eyes of a madman.

"Let her go, Colonel," Del ordered. "And maybe I won't kill you."

"Del?" Elisa cried.

"Wrong," Sanchez yelled. "Drop your weapon and come out, and maybe I won't kill her."

"Del, no!"

He wanted to go to her. Gather her up and tell her everything would be all right. But he couldn't. And it might not be.

He heard automatic gunfire from upstairs, and realized he wasn't going to get help from the paratroopers anytime soon.

Partially hidden by the door frame, he sighted his Hechler and Koch on the center of Sanchez's forehead, but Elisa was too close to risk a shot. Del had barely an inch as a margin of error.

"You drop her," he said, hoping his voice sounded more confident than he felt. "You've got no cover. I'll kill you before you before her body hits the floor."

Sanchez laughed demonically. "Then it looks like we have a standoff."

Del caught movement in the hallway off to Sanchez's right and a little in front of the colonel. Hope winged through his chest, and he smiled. "Tell you what," he proposed. "I'm only interested in the woman. You let her go, I'll let you go."

"You think I believe that?" He moved the pistol to Elisa's temple, dug the barrel in deep. She bit her lip, but held her silence. The movement in the side hall went still.

"It's the truth. You let her go, I'll let you walk right by me. Look." He lowered his pistol an inch. "I'll put my gun down if you lower yours. We'll do it together, an inch at a time so neither of us gets the drop on the other."

"Del, no! You cannot let him escape."

Difficult as it was, Del ignored her. He lowered his pistol another inch. "Come on. A little at a time. Just ease the gun away from her, and I'll put mine down."

Del held his breath, watching for any sign of cooperation. Slowly the colonel's hand dropped. Maybe half an inch.

"That's good," Del encouraged. He lowered his gun again. "Now you. A little more."

They played the game until Del's pistol rested on the floor, still cupped in his hand. The colonel's weapon hung at his side.

Still pulling Elisa with him, he shuffled forward a step. Then another. One more put him directly in line with the intersecting hall.

A figure leaped out of the shadows. Del's gun was up again in a flash, but he didn't need it. The young Hispanic man made a tackle on Sanchez that would have made a pro linebacker proud. A second young man caught Elisa as she spun away.

Pulling out plastic restraints, Del ran down the stairs to secure their prize.

Elisa pulled back from the man who'd caught her to

look at his face. Then she flung herself back into his arms. "Miguel? What are you doing here, my brother?"

Del put his foot on Sanchez's throat, and the man who'd tackled him backed away. "What about me? Don't I get a hug, big sister?"

"Raul! How did you know…?"

"Your ranger friend paid us a little visit," Raul answered.

"Along with a few dozen American soldiers," Miguel added ruefully.

Raul hung his thumbs in the waistband of his pants and arched his back. "Seems they needed a little help with their invasion."

"It's not an invasion, it's an extradition," Miguel said. "And all they needed was intelligence."

Raul cuffed him on the back of the head. "Then why did they ask you?"

Miguel rolled his eyes. "We gave them the layout of the house. But only if they let us come along."

Del smiled at the reunion as he finished securing the colonel's hands and feet.

Sanchez sneered up at Del. "Go ahead, Americano. Kill me. I spit in your face with my dying breath."

"Kill you? And deny your right to a fair trial and to spend the next fifty or sixty years rotting in an American prison? Not a chance, Colonel."

Finally ready for a reunion of his own, he stood.

But Elisa bent over the fallen paratrooper. "He is still alive. Miguel, find something to use as a pressure bandage. Search these rooms." She waved down the hall, then pulled off the trooper's headset. "Raul, figure out how this works and call for help."

"No need," Del said. He spoke quietly but urgently

into his own set and listened for the reply. "They're on the way."

Everything moved at light speed after that. The paratroopers arrived and then the regular infantry. Medics carried the wounded man away, while other soldiers carted Sanchez off under heavy guard. Elisa was removed to "debrief" with two men in suits. They had to be spooks, Del figured. Nobody but spooks wore suits to a raid. An American lieutenant asked Del to help round up Sanchez's key officers.

Much to his great displeasure, Del's reunion would have to wait.

Chapter 16

Other than the past two weeks, and a few short educational trips, Elisa had spent her entire life in San Ynez. Yet tonight the sight of the dark mountains charging up to the sky, the pattern of the stars overhead, the scent of the nearby rainforest were all unfamiliar. Foreign.

San Ynez no longer felt like home.

Elisa sat in the darkened doorway of an American military helicopter, watching the hubbub around Sanchez's mansion incredulously. She still could not believe the Americans had arrested Colonel Sanchez. In his own country.

But she was glad. And proud. For her people, and for theirs.

A man walked toward her in the distance. It was too dark to make out his face, but she recognized Del immediately. His shape. His walk. It was as if she had always known him. Always been a part of him. And him a part of her.

"Hey," he said, when he reached her.

"Hey." She should come up with something more articulate, but words for this moment escaped her.

"They said they had a doctor look at you."

She laid a hand on her belly. "We are fine. Clint?" she asked, suddenly picturing the ranger writhing on the ground as Sanchez's men had dragged her away.

"He's okay. Practically had to sedate him to keep him from coming along on this mission. Are you sure you're all right? And the baby?"

She took his hand, laid the broad palm over her stomach.

He frowned. "Am I supposed to feel something?"

"Not yet." She smiled and gently pressed her right side with her own hand. The baby kicked like a World Cup soccer star. Del's eyes widened. "We have learned a new trick since we have been away."

"So I see. Does it hurt?"

"No. Want me to do it again?"

"No!" He snapped his hand back. "I mean, maybe you'd better not. Let the poor girl rest."

Elisa laughed, fingered the silver circle and star pinned to his shirt. "Your Texas Ranger badge."

"A lot's happened since you disappeared. I got my job back, for one." She nodded towards the soldier scurrying about. "And started your own army for another?"

"Nope, these are the real deal. U.S. Special Forces."

"And they're here because...?"

He chuckled and relayed what Mr. "Bradford" had told him. "Without the gun deal, the State Department had no grounds for the extradition warrant on Sanchez," he added. But you had applied for your I-9 residency status before you were taken. Gene Randolph came up with the idea. He had State push your application through. We had a witness who saw you forcibly taken from the parking garage and a federal agent undercover in Sanchez's organization who could place you here in the compound.'' He grinned. ''Kidnapping a legal American resident is a serious offense. You provided grounds for the extradition.''

She was still sorting through everything he had said, trying to process it all, when he cupped her jaw in his palm, stroked his thumb across her cheek.

''It's over,'' he said.

Elisa's heart twisted even as she tipped her head back under the pleasure of his touch. ''Sanchez's reign of terror? Or our marriage?''

Del let her go, swung around and sat beside her. He looked at the ground between his feet. ''Sanchez is gone, and Herrerra will be reinstated as president—''

Elisa's head snapped up. ''Presidente Herrerra? But he is dead...''

''Not so dead after all. Seems his elite guard got word there might be an attempt on his yacht. They took him off the boat in time. He's been hiding out in the U.S. with a few of his men.''

''Eduardo,'' Elisa said, seeing the truth in her heart.

''Yeah. Eduardo.''

Her eyes burned. ''He was not a traitor.''

''He was a hero. He stayed loyal to Herrerra all those years, and eventually worked with the State Department to put him back in power. Herrerra is planning a special award for him, to be presented posthumously.''

Elisa touched her abdomen again. ''I am glad. For her sake.''

''Me, too. And for yours.''

The silence stretched uncomfortably between them.

Del cleared his throat. "Guess you can stay in San Ynez now, if you want. It's safe."

"Yes." The possibility should have made her happy. Instead an overwhelming sense of loss engulfed her.

What else had she expected? The ranger had married her out of a sense of duty. To protect her. Now he knew that he had not killed Eduardo, and her safety in San Ynez was not in question. His duty had been fulfilled, and so he was letting her go. Gently, as was his way.

"Of course," he said. "I don't know as there's going to be much need for a resistance leader here anymore."

"It is a job I will happily relinquish."

"What will you do?"

She pondered a moment. "Have this baby. Then help get the country back on its feet, I guess. Stabilize the economy. Promote trade agreements."

"With the U.S.?"

"Yes."

He shifted restlessly. "Maybe you'll have some business in the States?"

"Maybe."

"Or maybe…" He looked at her sideways, and Elisa didn't think she'd ever seen more fear on his face. "Maybe you could do what you need to do from the U.S."

Elisa's heart ricocheted off her breastbone. "Perhaps."

The ranger dug in his pocket, pulled out a slip of paper and handed it to her. "I told you State pushed through your residency application."

"My green card?" she asked, astonished.

"'Course, you probably don't want to leave your family, and there's a lot to do here."

Before she got too carried away, she had to be clear.

"Are you asking me to come back to the United States, or to come back to you?"

His jaw set stubbornly, and she realized just how much she had hurt him that last day. "You said you didn't want me to come looking for you…"

"I was an idiot. That's why I went to the courthouse, to tell you I was wrong and I was sorry. But I never got the chance."

Starlight gleamed off the intensity in his eyes. "Then come back to *me,* Elisa. And I'm not asking out of duty or obligation or debt. Come back to me because I love you. I love everything about who you are and who you've been. Come back because I want to marry you again, in a church this time, and raise this baby and three or four more with you."

Elisa nearly floated out of her skin. She let him suffer for…about a millisecond. Which was as long as she could hold herself back from throwing her arms around his neck and kissing every square inch of his face.

A few soldiers drifted by, storing gear. Some of them cast lingering, curious glances at them.

"And your family," she said into his neck, "they will accept this, knowing what they must know about me by now?"

He pulled back so he could see her. "I had a long talk with them before I left for this mission. You know what my Papi said?"

She shook her head.

Del grinned. "Said during World War Two he met a woman who ran a part of the French resistance. I think maybe they had something going, by the way. That was before he met Mami. Anyway, he said she was the bravest, smartest, most principled person he'd ever met. And he said you reminded him of her. He'd be Goddamn proud—''

He paused while Elisa crossed herself and mumbled a short prayer.

''—to have a woman like you in the family. Permanently. So will you marry me again, Elisa?''

She looped her arms around his neck and kissed him perfunctorily. ''I'll marry you again, Delgado Cooper. And again and again and again and—''

He cut her off with another kiss.

And this one was anything but perfunctory.

At the sound of clapping and whistling, Elisa raised her hand. The soldiers had formed a semicircle around them, a respectable distance away. A few shouted encouragement to Del, and he pulled her close, squeezing her almost painfully.

She thought back over all that had happened in the past two weeks. The people she'd met—Gene Randolph and Bull Matheson, Clint Hayes and even Kat Solomon and the soldiers here she hadn't met but who had saved her life.

They were all heroes.

But her gaze was inexorably drawn back to Del.

He might not be the last honorable man, she realized. But as far as she was concerned he was the best.

* * * * *

Anything. Anywhere. Anytime.

The crew of this C-17 squadron will leave you breathless!

WINGMEN WARRIORS

Catherine Mann's

edge-of-your-seat series continues in June with

PRIVATE MANEUVERS

First Lieutenant Darcy Renshaw flies headfirst into a dangerous undercover mission with handsome CIA agent Max Keegan, and the waters of Guam soon engulf them in a world of secrets, lies and undeniable attraction.

Don't miss this compelling installment available in June from

Silhouette

I N T I M A T E   M O M E N T S™

Available at your favorite retail outlet.

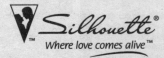
Silhouette®
Where love comes alive™

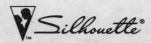

COMING NEXT MONTH